Dunces Anonymous

Kate Jaimet

DISCARDED

ORCA BOOK PUBLISHERS

Library and Archives Canada Cataloguing in Publication

Jaimet, Kate, 1969-
Dunces anonymous / written by Kate Jaimet.

ISBN 978-1-55469-097-8

I. Title.
PS8619.A368D86 2009   JC813'.6   C2009-903351-8

First published in the United States, 2009
Library of Congress Control Number: 2009929364

Summary: Josh forms a club to help kids whose parents have unrealistic
expectations of them and, in the process, learns what it really means to be a leader.

Mixed Sources
Product group from well-managed forests,
controlled sources and recycled wood or fiber
www.fsc.org Cert no. SW-COC-000952
© 1996 Forest Stewardship Council

*Orca Book Publishers is dedicated to preserving the environment and has printed this book
on paper certified by the Forest Stewardship Council.*

Orca Book Publishers gratefully acknowledges the support for its publishing
programs provided by the following agencies: the Government of Canada
through the Canada Book Fund and the Canada Council for the Arts,
and the Province of British Columbia through the BC Arts Council
and the Book Publishing Tax Credit.

Design by Teresa Bubela
Cover image by Dreamstime
Author photo by Mark Purves

ORCA BOOK PUBLISHERS   ORCA BOOK PUBLISHERS
PO Box 5626, Stn. B   PO Box 468
Victoria, BC Canada   CUSTER, WA USA
V8R 6S4   98240-0468

www.orcabook.com
Printed and bound in Canada.

13 12 11 10 • 5 4 3 2

To my writing group. I couldn't have done it without you.

CONTENTS

ONE

A CUNNING PLAN

Josh tapped a small wooden mallet on the teacher's desk. The clock on the wall read 12:03. The classroom was nearly deserted.

Josh's mallet sounded as faint as an ant stamping its tiny foot. The noise barely rose above the wall clock's electric hum.

Josh stared out at the classroom. Rows of empty desks stared back. In the far corner, Wang Xiu sat with his nose in a comic book. Two rows from the front, Magnolia Montcrieff was studying *Romeo and Juliet*. Had they stayed here for his meeting, or were they just lingering for some quiet reading while the other kids rushed to the cafeteria and Mr. Bogg vanished into the staff room for lunch?

"Um, you guys, could we get the meeting started?" Josh said.

Magnolia's head remained bent over her book. Wang's nose stayed buried in his comic. Josh twiddled his mallet. What was he supposed to do now?

He didn't have a clue.

Josh didn't know Wang and Magnolia very well. He didn't know anyone at Oakview Public School very well. He had only started there at the end of last year, after his parents split up. His dad had moved away and his mom bought a condo in a new part of town. He wasn't sure he'd get along with Wang and Magnolia, even if he did manage to get their attention. Still, here he was, standing at the front of the class, so he screwed up his courage and tapped the mallet on the desk again.

"Um, excuse me? I'd like to get the meeting started?"

Nobody heard him. Or, if they heard him, nobody listened. Josh sat down at Mr. Bogg's desk and sank his head in his arms. It was hopeless. He should have known it when he'd tacked his little sign to the class-room bulletin board that morning.

Today at Noon! First Meeting of Dunces Anonymous! A Club for Kids who aren't as Good at Stuff as their Parents Think they Should Be.

Who would want to join a club called Dunces Anonymous? It was a dumb name. It was a dumb idea. It was a dumb club. But what else could he do? He needed help. Josh was in terrible trouble, and he couldn't think of a way out of it by himself.

He'd been sitting there for about a minute, picturing his life going down the tubes at the age of eleven-and-a-half, when he felt a hand on his shoulder.

"What's wrong?"

He looked up and saw Magnolia standing next to him. She was a funny-looking girl, and for a moment her appearance distracted Josh from his problems. She was wearing multicolored overalls, and her short black hair was pinned up with dozens of little clips and barrettes so that it stood in tufts all over her head.

"What's wrong?" Magnolia demanded again.

"This meeting," said Josh. "It's a complete flop."

"Well," said Magnolia, "there are two of us here. Plus you, makes three. So it can't be a *complete* flop."

"It's not very good for someone who's supposed to be class president," said Josh.

"Who says you're supposed to be class president?"

"My mother," Josh moaned. "Don't you get it? That's why I called this meeting!"

"Well, how can I get it if you haven't told me anything? Sheesh!" said Magnolia.

Josh felt her slip the little wood mallet out of his hand. Then he heard a loud, crisp *crack* as she banged it on the desk.

"Hey! This meeting will now come to order! Everyone here for the Dunces Anonymous meeting, please come forward. Pronto!"

Wang lifted his nose from his comic book and came over to join them.

"Right," said Magnolia. "Now, Josh, tell us all about it."

Josh looked at the girl. Then he looked at the mallet in her hand. How had she done that? A person who could do that was the kind of person who should be class president. Class president. The feeling of hopelessness welled up again in Josh's stomach.

"Well," he began, "my mom's making me run for class president."

"And you want us to help you win," Magnolia interrupted.

"No! I want you to help me lose! I mean, I really, really don't want to be class president!"

Josh looked at the others, afraid they'd think he was dumb for not wanting to be class president. But they weren't laughing. Instead they looked interested.

"What does a class president do, anyway?" Wang asked. He had put his comic book down and was perched on a corner of Mr. Bogg's desk, swinging one foot back and forth.

What did a class president do? Josh wasn't totally sure. All he knew was that he didn't want to be one. His mom was the president of lots of different committees, and sometimes she dragged him along to her meetings. While he did his homework, the grown-ups talked for hours about boring things. It looked like an awful way to spend his first full year at a new school.

"I think they have to organize things," Josh said.

"That's right," said Magnolia. "Like bake sales and Halloween parties and bottle drives, and even letter-writing campaigns to free political prisoners and stuff."

Josh groaned. That sounded even worse than he'd thought.

"But why do you need us to help you lose the election?" Wang said. "No offense, but you could probably lose on your own."

"I thought of that," said Josh, "but the only other person running is Stacey Hogarth!"

"Oh." Wang's foot stopped swinging. "That's a problem."

"I knew it!" Josh wailed. "Nobody's going to vote for Stacey Hogarth. I'm doomed. Doomed!"

A sharp rapping sound brought Josh up short. Magnolia was banging the mallet on Mr. Bogg's desk again and looking at him with a deep frown.

"Now, Josh!" she scolded. "Crying about it is not going to do you any good!"

"Why don't you run for class president, Magnolia?" Josh said. "I bet you'd beat me by a million votes."

Magnolia cocked her head, as though considering his idea, and for a moment Josh thought his problem was solved. But then she shook her head.

"Sorry, I can't. My mom would kill me. She wants me to *devote* myself *completely* to playing Juliet in the school play." Magnolia rolled her eyes.

"Oh," said Josh. He had the feeling that Magnolia expected him to say something more, but he wasn't sure what it could be.

"Which I *do not* want to do!" Magnolia added.

"Oh," said Josh again. He was confused. They hadn't solved his presidential problem yet, but now they had switched to talking about the school play. It was like the meetings his mom took him to. Even when she told him to pay attention, he could never keep track of what was going on, and the conversation always seemed to wander off in different directions.

"Do you want me to tell you all about it?" said Magnolia.

"I guess so," said Josh.

"Well." Magnolia stepped back and let out a deep sigh. "When my mother was a little girl, she dreamed of being a romantic star of stage and screen. But her father disapproved and never allowed her to take acting lessons. Now she wants me to fulfill her shattered dreams!"

"Don't you like acting?" asked Josh. She seemed pretty dramatic for someone who didn't want to be a romantic star of stage and screen.

"I love acting! But not the mushy stuff." Magnolia clutched her hands to her heart. "'Oh, Romeo, Romeo, wherefore art thou, Romeo!' Sheesh! Give me a break!"

"Pretty bad," Josh agreed.

Wang nodded.

"Yeah," Magnolia said, "but when I tried telling my mom that I didn't want to be Juliet, she started crying. You should have heard her. 'I dreamed of playing Juliet when I was a girl! I shut myself in my room and wept when my father wouldn't let me take acting lessons! You have no idea how lucky you are!'"

Josh nodded sympathetically. He knew from experience that it was impossible to win an argument with a crying mother.

"What we need," said Wang, "is a cunning plan." He tapped the cover of his comic book. "Superheroes always have a cunning plan."

"What kind of a cunning plan?" asked Magnolia.

"Beats me," Wang admitted. "I'm no good at cunning plans. If I were, I wouldn't be stuck in the chess club."

"What does the chess club have to do with anything?" Josh asked. He was feeling lost again.

"That's why I came to this meeting," Wang explained. "Isn't that what your notice said? '*A club for kids who aren't as good at stuff as their parents think they should be*'? Well, that's me. See, last year, my dad made me join the chess club. I was getting Cs in school, and he said chess was supposed to help me concentrate and improve my grades. I didn't win a single game all year, and I'm still getting Cs, but my dad won't let me quit. He says, 'A quitter never succeeds.' But how is doing something I hate going to help me succeed?"

Josh shook his head. Parents didn't make any sense. But what could a kid do about it? He looked at the clock. It was already twelve thirty and they hadn't solved a single one of their problems.

"We need to prioritize," said Magnolia. "The election for class president is tomorrow, so we need to help Josh first. Now, who's got a cunning plan to help him lose the election?"

Josh looked at Wang. Wang looked down at his comic book.

"Maybe there's something in there," Josh suggested timidly.

"I don't think so," said Wang. "Superheroes always have plans for winning battles—not for losing."

"Winning an election's easy," Josh said. His mother had told him so a million times. "You have to promise people all the things they want. Like longer recesses and field trips to the swimming pool and class parties every Friday."

"Well, then," said Wang, "all you have to do is make a speech tomorrow, promising kids all the things they *don't* want."

Josh and Magnolia looked at each other. The idea was brilliant. Cunning, even.

"You mean, like, study groups during recess?" Josh ventured.

"Yeah!" Wang said. "And detentions for anyone who makes a mistake on a test. And no French fries in the cafeteria! Only Brussels sprouts and lima beans!"

"It's perfect," Josh whispered.

"It just might work," said Magnolia.

"My friends," said Wang, "glorious defeat is within our grasp!"

He rolled up his comic book and waved it above his head like a sword.

"Onward, Dunces Anonymous!"

TWO

DOWN WITH JOSH!

Josh had spent the evening with Wang and Magnolia, writing his speech and drawing a campaign poster on a piece of blue bristol board. Now he was back in Mr. Bogg's classroom, with his speech clutched in his sweaty hand and the poster taped to the blackboard for everyone to see.

Vote for Veggies! Josh for President! the poster said. Around the border, Wang had doodled some flying carrots and green peppers in superhero capes. They looked pretty cool, Josh thought glumly.

Next to Josh's campaign poster hung Stacey Hogarth's. It was laser-printed and featured a big photo of Stacey's face. Her campaign slogan was *Progressive! Proactive! Professional! Hogarth for President!*

Josh looked around the classroom. Two guys in the back were tossing a mini football. A cluster of kids was jostling each other in a rock-paper-scissors showdown. A girl was playing space aliens on her cell phone. Another girl was bopping her head to the tunes on her MP3 player, and flipping through a fashion magazine. Would these kids be more likely to vote for someone *Progressive*, *Proactive* and *Professional*, or someone who had cool-looking superhero veggies doodled on his poster?

Josh let out a sigh. He had a sinking feeling that doodled veggies would carry the day.

Finally, Mr. Bogg brought the class to order and called Josh forward to give his speech. He cleared his throat as he walked to the front of the class, his speech clenched in his fist. His mother had told him to start off with a zinger—a quick, zippy line that would tell everyone what he stood for. A line that no one would forget. As he turned to face the classroom, Josh realized he had forgotten his zinger.

He looked down at the crumpled, sweat-smeared paper in his hand. Then he looked back up at the class.

"Lima beans!" he said.

The kids looked confused. Josh swallowed hard and continued reading. "Did you know that lima beans are a good source of cholesterol-lowering fiber? Or that half a cup of boiled lima beans provides one hundred percent of your daily requirement of molbydum... moldybum...molybdenum? Lima beans also supply your body with protein, potassium and vitamin B1! And yet, fellow students, the school cafeteria does not serve lima beans! If you elect me president, I will take French fries off the cafeteria's menu and substitute lima beans!"

Josh paused and looked up, searching for a reaction from the class. Most of the kids looked at him blankly. Then a boy named Eric, whose parents had sent him to fat camp over the summer, began to applaud. A skinny vegan girl named Mona started clapping too. Josh shot a desperate glance at Magnolia. Taking her cue, she jumped up from her seat.

"Boo!" she shouted. "Boo! No lima beans!"

Mr. Bogg rose from his desk. He was a very tall man with a bald, domed head. A blue vein bulged at his temple. "Magnolia!" he barked.

"I was just expressing my democratic opinion, sir."

"You can express it when the time comes to vote. Now sit down and be quiet."

"Yes, sir." Magnolia slid back into her seat with a sheepish look.

Josh shot her a grateful glance. Then he looked down at his scrunched-up speech and carried on.

"Secondly, a lot of people complain that we have too much homework."

Josh saw some kids nodding their heads, so he spoke quickly. "But that's not true! Homework is essential for scholastic achievement!" He'd borrowed that line from his mother. It was sure to go over badly.

"In fact, the problem is, we just don't have enough time to do our homework," Josh continued. "So if you elect me president, I'll cancel recess and replace it with a study period instead!"

This time Magnolia didn't wait for anyone to applaud. She sprang to her feet immediately.

"Boo! Bad idea! Boo!"

"Boo!" Wang joined in. "We want recess! Boo!"

"Magnolia! Wang!" Mr. Bogg hollered, slamming a ruler on his desk. "One more interruption and you'll both be going to the principal's office!"

"Yes, sir." Magnolia slunk back into her chair.

"Josh, please carry on."

"Finally," Josh continued, speaking quickly to get things over with, "if you elect me president, I'll abolish the class Halloween and Christmas parties and replace them with homework periods instead. And," he added in a flash of inspiration, "I'll replace all the Halloween candy with lima beans!"

"Boo! Boo!" This time Magnolia jumped onto her chair, shouting and waving her arms. "Down with Josh! Down with Josh!"

"Down with Josh!" Wang echoed, pounding on his desk.

"Magnolia! Wang!" Mr. Bogg thundered. But it was too late. The entire class had taken up the chant. "Down with Josh! Down with Josh! Down with Josh!" they yelled.

Mr. Bogg rose like an angry giant. The large blue vein in his temple throbbed.

"Magnolia Montcrieff! Get down off that chair and march yourself to the principal's office immediately! You too, Wang Xiu!" Mr. Bogg boomed. The class fell silent. Magnolia climbed down from the chair and hung her head. At her seat in the front row, Stacey Hogarth smirked.

Mr. Bogg stood with his hands on his hips as Wang and Magnolia filed toward the classroom door. As she passed Josh, Magnolia lifted her head just enough to flash him a quick grin. She was out the door before

Josh could smile back, but he felt a tear of gratitude spring to his eye. It took true friends to shout "Down with Josh!" so loudly and convincingly. It was good to know he had such friends.

Josh was late getting home that evening. He felt it was a point of honor to wait in the schoolyard until Wang and Magnolia finished their detentions, and to give a bus ticket to Wang, who had missed the school bus. By the time Josh swiped his pass-card to get into the front door of his mom's condo building, the lobby was already full of adults coming home from work. The lobby had shiny marble floors and two elevators with gold-colored doors, and Josh hated it. He liked the house they had lived in before the divorce. It was an ordinary house with swings in the backyard and a rec room in the basement. The kind of house where families with kids lived. As far as he could tell, he was the only kid who lived in his mom's condo building.

A knot of adults stood in front of the elevators, waiting for the doors to open. The men were dressed in suits and ties. The women wore jackets and skirts and high-heeled shoes. Some of them were talking on cell phones while they gripped briefcases or laptop-computer bags. They all looked as if they had been class presidents when they were kids. Josh veered away from them and headed up the back staircase toward the sixth floor.

In the kitchen, his mother was making supper and talking on the phone. Josh snuck up behind her and stole a carrot slice from the salad she was making. "I just don't think we can move forward under those parameters, Jen," Mom was saying. *Move forward under those parameters*—that was how class presidents were supposed to talk. He didn't know exactly what it meant, but from the tone of his mom's voice, it sounded like a fancy way of saying no.

Josh set the table while his mom finished talking on the phone. Then he held the plates while she dished out the supper, which was some kind of chicken with orange slices and pieces of crushed burnt nuts on top. Mom always cooked supper from scratch. "I'm not about to shirk my family responsibilities just because I have a career," she'd say. His dad had a different attitude. "Cook my own dinner? What, and put all the pizza joints out of business?" Josh had eaten a lot of takeout when he'd stayed with his dad last summer.

Mom's eyes sparkled as they sat down at the table. He could tell she was excited about the class election.

"So," she said, "am I speaking to the new president?"

"No, I lost." Josh tried to sound disappointed.

"Oh, Josh!" Mom looked at him like he'd just dropped an expensive dinner plate. "What happened? Did you flub your speech?"

Josh shrugged. The speech had gone brilliantly. But how could he explain that to his mom?

"Stacey Hogarth won."

"Stacey Hogarth!" His mother pursed her lips. "I know her mother from the Women's Business Council. Those Hogarths are all the same."

Not like us Johnsons, thought Josh. No one ever told him he was just like his mother. Was that a good thing or a bad thing? Josh couldn't decide, so he picked up his knife and fork and tackled his supper. If he scraped off all the nuts and oranges, he discovered, it was ordinary chicken underneath. Josh didn't mind eating ordinary chicken; in fact, he liked ordinary chicken. That was his mom though—she'd never serve ordinary chicken for supper. Just like she didn't want him to be ordinary Josh—he had to be Josh, the class president.

"Don't worry, Mom," he said, trying to cheer her up. "I started a new club at school and guess what? I'm the president."

"Well, that's good," said his mother. "What's the club called?"

"Dun…" He caught himself just in time. Mom would flip if she knew he'd started a club called Dunces Anonymous. He took a big gulp of milk to give himself time to think.

"Dunno yet," he said. "It's just a club where kids can get together and talk about, you know, their ambitions for the future."

Ambitions for the future. Mom would like that, and it wasn't *exactly* a lie.

"That sounds great, honey," Mom said. "You could call it Young Leaders of the Future."

Josh gagged on his chicken. That was exactly what he *wouldn't* call it.

"Yeah, maybe," he mumbled. "I'd have to ask the other kids in the club."

His mother smiled.

"Democracy is good, honey," she said, "but a leader has to lead."

Josh stared back at his mom. Sometimes he didn't get her. If a leader has to lead, why was she always trying to boss him around?

"Well, good for you, honey, for landing on your feet!" his mother continued, spearing another piece of chicken. "Young Leaders of the Future. I'll have to tell Stacey Hogarth's mother about it the next time I see her."

"No! Don't tell her...," Josh protested. His mother interrupted him.

"Now, Josh, you shouldn't be so modest about your accomplishments. Right?" She reached over and lifted his chin. "Right?"

"Right, Mom," Josh mumbled. She smiled and kept eating, but Josh could barely choke down another bite of his chicken, even with the nuts scraped off. Why had he said anything to his mom?

If his mom talked to Stacey's mom, Stacey's mom would talk to Stacey. And if Stacey thought Josh had started a Leadership club, she'd want to join—that's the kind of girl Stacey was.

But they couldn't let Stacey join Dunces Anonymous. If she did, she'd ruin everything.

THREE

MONTAGUES AND CATAPULTS

"*Romeo and Juliet*! Sheesh!" Magnolia plucked the book from her backpack and flung it emphatically onto her mother's favorite floral armchair.

The gesture was completely lost on Josh and Wang. The two boys had taken over the red velvet sofa and were madly thumbing a pair of video-game remote controls, filling the Montcrieffs' living room with gunshots and explosions. Magnolia picked up the master remote and clicked off the TV.

"Hey! We were just about to get to level nine!" Wang protested.

"I thought we were having a meeting!" said Magnolia.

"Oh, yeah. Sorry," said Josh.

"Well, we'd better get down to it," said Magnolia. "The auditions for the school play are this Friday. What are we going to do?"

Josh glanced nervously at the swinging door that led from the living room into the kitchen.

"Don't you think we should keep our voices down?" he said.

Magnolia had to admit that her living room wasn't the best place in the world to hold a meeting, what with two parents and three nosy younger brothers running around the house. But that bossy Stacey Hogarth had taken over Mr. Bogg's classroom for her Bake Sale Organizing Committee right after she was elected president, and there was no place else for them to go.

Magnolia had warned her two middle brothers, Randy and Robin, to stay out of the living room. But she couldn't very well stop her mother from cooking supper in the kitchen. From behind the swinging door came the blabber of the kitchen television set and the banging of pots and pans. While she cooked, Magnolia's mom always watched her favorite soap opera, *Young Hearts Afire*.

"Don't worry," said Magnolia. "She doesn't hear *anything* when her show is on."

"I heard that, sweetheart!" Magnolia's mom burst through the swinging door, carrying a plate of cookies. Garland, the youngest of Magnolia's brothers, trailed behind her, clinging with one hand to her gauzy, flowered dress. He was reaching out his free hand and babbling, "Tookie! Tookie!" Their mom was paying no attention.

Magnolia's mom liked to say that little boys were like zucchini vines: the best thing to do was just let them grow. Girls, on the other hand, were like delicate flowers: they had to be nurtured and cultivated. Sometimes, Magnolia wished she had been born a zucchini vine so that she could get on with her life.

"I think it's so lovely when Magnolia has friends over!" her mom exclaimed, setting down the plate of cookies on top of a pile of celebrity gossip magazines on the coffee table. "Did you boys come to help her with the audition?"

"Um, something like that," said Josh, biting into a cookie.

"Did Magnolia tell you that I dreamed of playing Juliet when I was a girl?"

She lifted a hand to her forehead and recited, "'In fair Verona, where we set our scene, a pair of star-crossed lovers take their life!'"

"Star-crossed lovers! Sheesh!" Magnolia rolled her eyes.

"Never underestimate the power of true love, sweetheart." Magnolia's mom sighed. "You are a beautiful flower in the bloom of your youth! Enjoy it! Enjoy every moment!"

That sounded like a dramatic exit line if Magnolia ever heard one, and sure enough, her mom swept out of the room, back to the saga of *Young Hearts Afire*. Little Garland was left behind in the living room, trying to pull down the pile of magazines so that he could reach the cookie plate. Magnolia scooped up her baby brother and set him on some cushions in a corner with a couple of cookies to keep him happy. Then she turned back to the boys.

"Honestly, you guys, do I look like a star-crossed lover?"

She held out her arms so they could see how much she *didn't* look like a star-crossed lover. She was wearing plaid pants and a fake zebra-fur jacket that she'd found at a thrift shop.

"Not really," said Wang.

"Not exactly," said Josh.

"Not at all! Sheesh! What am I going to do?" Magnolia flung herself backward, landing, arms outstretched, in the floral armchair.

"Maybe," Josh piped up timidly, "you could just flub your lines?"

Magnolia frowned but didn't answer. Actually, she'd already thought of that. If she flubbed her lines, obviously she wouldn't get the part. But the solution seemed so dramatically unsatisfying. Anyone could flub their lines! It didn't take an actress to do that! And Magnolia was a serious actress. Last year, she had played Schoolgirl Number Three in the television miniseries of *Anne of Green Gables*. The part of Anne had been taken by a natural redhead. You couldn't fight typecasting.

"I know!" said Wang. "What if you were suddenly paralyzed?"

"Paralyzed?" said Magnolia.

"By stage fright," Josh suggested.

Paralyzed by stage fright! It had dramatic possibilities. Magnolia rose from the armchair.

"I walk on stage," she began, acting out the idea as she thought it through. "Suddenly, the glare of the lights hits me. I freeze." Magnolia froze. "My mind is a blank! I can't remember why I'm here! I can't remember what play

I'm auditioning for! My ears are filled with a buzzing...no, no, a ringing sound! My hand begins to shake." She held out her hand. It was trembling. "Suddenly I feel faint! The room begins to spin! I fall to the ground!"

Magnolia let her knees crumple beneath her. She was aiming to collapse onto the carpet in the narrow space between the television set and the coffee table, but as she swooned, her outstretched hand hit the pile of magazines on the table and sent the plate of cookies flying.

"Tookie! Tookie!" Garland screamed. The kitchen door flew open.

"Magnolia! What's happening?" her mother exclaimed. She rushed to the place where Magnolia lay on the ground, eyes half-closed.

"Oh! You're rehearsing the death scene!" her mother cried.

Magnolia heard a thump on the carpet as her mom fell to her knees beside her.

"'What's here? A cup clos'd in my true love's hand?" her mother excalimed. "Poison, I see, hath been his timeless end!'"

"Mom!" Magnolia tried to sit up, but her mother pushed her back to the floor.

"'Yea, a noise? Then I'll be brief! Oh, happy dagger, let me die!'"

Magnolia watched as her mother pretended to stab herself in the heart with an imaginary dagger. Then, before she could squirm out of the way, her mother collapsed on top of her in a flowery heap that smelled of beef stroganoff.

"Mom! Get off me!"

But her mother wouldn't move until the dramatic moment was over. Magnolia stopped struggling and sank back into the carpet. Sheesh! If her mom wanted to play Juliet so badly, why didn't *she* audition for the part?

The school gymnasium was swarming with Juliets on the Friday afternoon of the auditions. Magnolia hadn't seen so much satin and crinoline in one place since her kindergarten's Halloween party, when all the other girls in the class had dressed up as princesses. Magnolia had worn a dragon costume. No such luck this time, she thought, as she tugged at the sleeves of the lacy, pale blue gown her mother had rented from the costume shop especially for this audition.

"I feel like Tinkerbell in a nightie," she muttered to Josh—not too loudly, because her mother was hovering nearby.

"Don't worry," Josh whispered back. "Remember: stage fright."

"Right." Magnolia nodded.

"Oh, Magnolia, did you see Emmett?" A girl burst through the crowd and appeared at Magnolia's elbow. She was wearing a long pink ball gown, and her blond hair was swept up beneath a silver tiara.

"Hi, Hannah," said Magnolia.

"Did you see him?" Hannah repeated, gesturing to a corner of the gym. "Isn't he gorgeous?"

Magnolia looked over to the corner, where a small knot of boys was standing around awkwardly, waiting for the auditions to start. They were all dressed in ordinary jeans and T-shirts. All except one. Emmett Blackwell. Emmett was wearing purple velvet pants and a shirt with ruffles down the front.

Emmett was one year ahead of her, in grade seven, but Magnolia knew him from the *Anne of Green Gables* miniseries. He had played the part of Gilbert, Anne's admirer, and Magnolia remembered how he'd strutted around the set like he was some big movie star. He wouldn't even talk to her because she was just Schoolgirl Number Three. No doubt he was auditioning for Romeo! She hoped he'd get the role of Third Gravedigger.

"He's wearing purple pants," Magnolia said to Hannah. How could anyone have a crush on a guy who wore purple pants?

"I think I'm going to faint!" Hannah moaned.

"Oh, give me a break!" said Magnolia. Before Hannah could carry through on her threat, Mrs. Karloff appeared on the stage at the front of the gymnasium. She clapped her hands for silence.

"All right, people!" she announced. "We'll start with the lead roles. Anyone wishing to audition for the parts of Romeo or Juliet, come backstage, now! Everyone else: Quiet in the house!"

Hannah grabbed Magnolia's hand and began dragging her toward the stage.

"Break a leg, darling!" Magnolia's mother called after her.

"Break two!" shouted Wang, grinning.

Easy for him to say. He didn't have to fake an attack of stage fright in front of his own mother. Maybe I really will get stage fright, thought Magnolia, starting to feel nervous. Wouldn't that take the cake?

"All right, quiet down!" Mrs. Karloff commanded, as the last of the Juliets straggled into the wings. Mrs. Karloff was dressed all in black, with a chunky necklace of glass and wooden beads around her neck and a black beret on her head. She wore the highest-heeled shoes that Magnolia had ever seen, and they rapped the stage like a conductor's baton, calling the actors to order.

"Now, for this audition, you're going to be playing the famous balcony scene. That's Act Two, Scene Two, if you'd all turn to that page in your scripts."

Mrs. Karloff gave everyone a moment to find the right page. "Okay, Romeo"—she turned to the boys—"you've just met Juliet at a party and you've fallen madly in love with her. There's only one problem. Your family, the Montagues, are the deadly enemies of her family, the Capulets. If your father knew you loved her, he'd kill both of you.

"Okay, Juliet"—she turned to the girls—"you've just met Romeo at a party and you've fallen madly in love with him. There's only one problem. Your family, the Capulets, are the deadly enemies of his family, the Montagues. If your father knew you loved him, he'd kill both of you. Right. Now in this scene, it's nighttime. Juliet, you can't sleep. You go out onto your balcony, thinking about how much you love Romeo.

"Romeo, you sneak into Juliet's garden, hoping to catch a glimpse of her. There she is on the balcony, a vision of beauty. You exchange your vows of true love. Think of the danger! Think of the passion!"

Mrs. Karloff looked down at the clipboard she was carrying. "All right! First up, we'll have Vincent Nguyen as Romeo and Hannah Flynn as Juliet. Hannah, you'll start at 'O Romeo, Romeo, wherefore art thou, Romeo?...' When you're ready!"

Mrs. Karloff strode off the stage, her high heels clacking down the stairs, and went to stand in the center of the gym floor to watch the audition.

Hannah squeezed Magnolia's hand.

"Wish me luck!" she whispered.

"Good luck!" said Magnolia. And she meant it. She was starting to feel a twinge of guilt about the trick she was going to play on her mother. Magnolia peeked out from behind the wings. There was her mom, sitting on a folding chair facing center stage, her hands clenched in her lap. Magnolia knew her mom would weep if she didn't get the part of Juliet—even if it was caused by an "innocent" case of stage fright. Why couldn't she understand that Magnolia didn't *want* to be a romantic heroine? But no, it would be Magnolia's fault for dashing her mother's hopes.

Maybe one of the other Juliets would pull off such a fantastic audition that Mrs. Karloff would award her the role on the spot. Then Magnolia wouldn't have to go through with the charade. She looked hopefully at Hannah, who was gliding onto the stage in her ball gown.

Hannah sure fit the part, with her long golden hair and her slim figure.

Even Vincent Nguyen, who was supposed to be playing Romeo, seemed suddenly too shy to approach her. One of the other Romeos had to shove him onto the stage. Hannah held her hand to her heart and gazed wistfully into the audience. Magnolia crossed her fingers tightly. Then Hannah opened her mouth to speak her first line.

"O Romeo, Romeo, werewolf art thou, Romeo?"

Bang! Mrs. Karloff's spiky heel came down hard on the gymnasium floor. The sound echoed around the room like a judge's gavel. Magnolia bit her lip.

"Hannah, darling, this is *Romeo and Juliet*, not *Twilight*!" Mrs. Karloff snapped. "It's 'Romeo, Romeo, *wherefore* art thou, Romeo!'"

"Oh." Hannah peered at the script. "Right."

"Try it again," Mrs. Karloff directed. "From the top!"

Hannah glanced back at Magnolia, who gave her the thumbs-up. Maybe it was a real case of stage fright, Magnolia thought. Maybe once she got started, Hannah would be okay.

Hannah put her hand to her heart and began again. "O Romeo, Romeo, wherefore art thou, Romeo? Denny thy father, and refuse thy name—"

"Stop! Stop!" Mrs. Karloff cried, stamping her heel again. "Hannah, darling, why do you say '*Denny* thy father,' when Shakespeare very clearly wrote '*Deny* thy father'? Don't you understand? Juliet is telling Romeo to deny his father, to forget about his father, because his father won't approve of their love!"

"Oh." Hannah looked at the script again. "I thought it was 'Denny, thy father.' You know, like his father's name was Denny."

"This is Shakespeare, darling," Mrs. Karloff sighed. "There are no Dennys in Shakespeare."

Hannah glanced nervously back at Magnolia. Magnolia forced herself to smile, but her hopes for Hannah's stage debut were rapidly sinking. Hannah took a deep breath and struck her pose again.

"O Romeo, Romeo, wherefore art thou, Romeo?
Deny thy father and refuse thy name.
Or, if thou wilt not, be but sworn my love,
And I'll no longer be a Catapult!"

A Catapult! Magnolia groaned.

"No! No! No!" Mrs. Karloff shouted, waving her arms and slamming her spiky-heeled shoes into the floor. "It's Capulet! Capulet! Not Catapult!"

"Capulet?" Hannah frowned.

"Yes. Of course. Juliet's family name is Capulet!" Mrs. Karloff sounded exasperated. "When she says to Romeo, 'I'll no longer be a Capulet,' it means she's willing to give up her family for the sake of his love!"

"Oh," said Hannah. "I thought it meant she was going to catapult someone off the balcony. This *is* the balcony scene, isn't it?"

Mrs. Karloff sighed and looked at her clipboard.

"All right, Hannah, thank you," she said. "Chelsea Laroque? Chelsea, please, you're next."

Magnolia gave Hannah's hand a squeeze when she came off the stage, but no amount of sympathy could change the fact that she'd blown her audition. Chelsea turned out to be even worse than Hannah, and the third Juliet was as bad as the first two put together. There was no other way out, Magnolia thought grimly. She'd have to put the stage-fright plan into action.

"Next up," Mrs. Karloff called. "Magnolia Montcrieff as Juliet. And as Romeo—Emmett Blackwell!"

Emmett Blackwell! Magnolia froze in her tracks. She hadn't reckoned on playing opposite Emmett. As he stepped forward onto the stage, she noticed that besides the purple pants and frilly shirt, Emmett was wearing a pair of shiny black shoes with brass buckles.

"I see you've put some thought in to your costume, Emmett," said Mrs. Karloff approvingly. "Well, come on, Magnolia. We haven't got all day."

Magnolia lifted her chin and stepped forward. Who did Emmett think he was anyway? Just because he played Gilbert in *Anne of Green Gables* and she was only Schoolgirl Number Three didn't mean that she couldn't share the stage with him. She was as good an actor as Emmett Blackwell, any day.

"Why don't you begin, Emmett?" Mrs. Karloff said. "We'll start at 'But soft! What light through yonder window breaks...' Go ahead when you're ready!"

Mrs. Karloff stood still, watching from her post in the gymnasium. Emmett took a few steps toward the back of the stage. Then he crouched down and snuck forward, as though he were creeping through the bushes of Juliet's garden. He stopped and looked up; then, in a voice that sounded like a whisper, yet somehow carried through the whole gymnasium, he said, "'But soft! What light through yonder window breaks? It is the east, and Juliet is the sun!'"

Total silence fell over the gym as Emmett continued his speech. Magnolia's mother gazed at him, enraptured. Magnolia felt herself getting angrier and angrier.

She couldn't possibly have an attack of stage fright now. She couldn't make herself look like a fool in front of Mister-Big-Shot-Actor Emmett Blackwell. She could feel her anger brimming over, and when the time came for her to deliver her first lines, her voice exploded from her throat.

"O Romeo, Romeo, wherefore art thou, Romeo?
Deny thy father and refuse thy name!
Or, if thou wilt not, be but sworn my love,
And I'll no longer be a Capulet!"

Magnolia paused to take a breath. She was surprised at how loud her voice sounded. The word *Capulet* still echoed in the gymnasium. Her mother was leaning forward in her chair, enthralled. But behind her mom, Josh and Wang were making wild gestures for Magnolia to shut up.

"Good, good, Magnolia!" Mrs. Karloff called out. "You're angry at your father! I can feel your anger! Carry on!"

Good? Magnolia thought. Carry on? This wasn't working out at all. She forced back her anger and uttered her next lines in a soft voice.

"'Tis but thy name that is my enemy,
Thou are thyself, though not a Montague.
O, be some other name belonging to a man!"

"Yes! Yes!" Mrs. Karloff interrupted again. "Your anger is gone now! You're thinking about how much you love him! Excellent, Magnolia!"

Excellent? No, this couldn't be happening! She didn't want to be excellent. She didn't want to be Emmett's Juliet. She choked out her next lines in a strangled voice:

"What's in a name? That which we call a rose
By any other word would smell as sweet.
So Romeo would, were he not Romeo called!"

"Bravo! Bravo! Fantastic!" Mrs. Karloff strode forward onto the stage. "Magnolia, darling! I can feel your despair!"

Despair is right, Magnolia thought, looking helplessly at Emmett Blackwell, whose face still wore the look of a love-struck Romeo. Somewhere backstage, Hannah burst into tears and ran off in a clatter of high-heeled shoes.

"People!" Mrs. Karloff announced, holding out her arms to Magnolia and Emmett. "Allow me to introduce you to Oakview Public School's new Romeo and Juliet!"

Magnolia's mother leaped from her chair and burst into applause. But Josh shook his head, and Wang fell to the floor in a mock faint.

What have I done? Magnolia thought. How am I going to get out of this now?

FOUR

ROMEO REHEARSES

It didn't take many rehearsals for Magnolia to figure out the worst part about playing Juliet. It wasn't the mushy dialogue or the floor-length dress she had to wear. The worst part was definitely the kissing.

Romeo kisses Juliet three times in Shakespeare's play: twice at the party in Act One and once during the death scene in Act Five. Emmett only pretended during rehearsals, of course, his lips swooping close to hers with a repulsive smacking sound. But by the second week of practice, a rumor was sweeping the school that on performance night Emmett intended to kiss Magnolia right on the mouth.

"Oh, Magnolia! Have you heard?" Hannah Flynn caught her by the sleeve backstage during rehearsal one afternoon.

"Heard what?" Magnolia said.

Hannah had volunteered to understudy the role of Juliet, but her main occupation seemed to be keeping up on the gossip about the cast.

"About performance night! Emmett's going to clasp you in his arms and hold you in a kiss of undying passion!"

"No, he's not," Magnolia said. "Not unless he wants a detention."

Oakview Public School had a strict policy about kisses of undying passion: They weren't allowed on school property. Even giving someone a peck on the cheek could get a kid sent to the principal's office.

"I heard he'd risk a whole week of detentions for the chance to kiss his Juliet right on the lips!" Hannah sighed. "Isn't it romantic?"

"It's ridiculous!" retorted Magnolia.

There had to be some way out of this dumb play. But how on earth was she going to get around her mother? Magnolia sidled away from Hannah and edged toward the stage curtain, where Josh was standing beside the pull-cord. He had volunteered as curtain-puller to stay close to the action, while they tried to think of a way for Magnolia to weasel out of the role of Juliet. Peeking around the curtain, Magnolia could see her mother sitting on a wooden chair right in front of the stage, wearing a cotton peasant skirt and a lot of flowery scarves draped around her neck. At her feet, Garland was stuffing his pudgy hands into her purse, pulling out keys, coins, credit cards and tissues, and scattering them all over the gym floor. Her mom didn't even seem to notice. She was leaning forward, mouthing the words of the Prologue along with the actor on the stage.

"'From forth the fatal loins of these two foes, a pair of star-crossed lovers take their life…'"

"She's driving me bonkers!" Magnolia muttered, leaning her back against the wall next to Josh.

"Maybe you could break your ankle," Josh suggested, keeping his voice low so as not to interrupt the rehearsal.

"Thanks," Magnolia whispered back. "I'll just go jump off a roof."

"Couldn't you fake it?" Josh whispered.

"You can't fool an X-ray machine, Josh."

"How about coming down with a fever? Or the flu?"

"A fever? The flu? Are you kidding? My mother would drag me out on that stage even if I had the bubonic plague." Magnolia clutched her hand to her heart, mimicking her mother. "Rise from your deathbed, daughter! The show must go on!"

Magnolia peeked around the curtain again. In the far corner of the gym, Wang and some other boys were practicing sword-fighting. When Josh had volunteered as curtain-puller, Wang had signed up to play one of the Capulets. The main job of the Capulets was to get into brawls with Romeo's relatives, the Montagues. Wang didn't have any lines, but he got to do a lot of fighting.

"Let's go see Wang," Magnolia whispered. She wasn't needed on stage for a while. "At least he looks like he's having fun."

In the corner, the guys were attacking each other with plastic swords, ducking and parrying and pretending to fall down dead. Why couldn't girls get parts like that? Magnolia thought bitterly.

"This is awesome," said Wang, demonstrating a lunge with his plastic sword as they approached. "You should sign up to be a Capulet, Josh!"

"No, thanks."

"Seriously, Josh, it's really cool." Wang performed some cuts and thrusts with his sword. "The kid who plays Tybalt is showing us all how to do it. He says I'm a natural. His dad's a fencing instructor—that's a kind of sword-fighting—and he's going to give us a free lesson on Saturday, and…oh!"

Wang stopped mid-thrust.

"What?" said Josh and Magnolia together.

"I've got a chess competition Saturday."

Wang sank to the floor in a lump of gloom.

"Couldn't you skip it?" Josh asked.

Wang shook his head.

"My dad would kill me."

"But you can't miss the sword-fighting lesson!" Magnolia turned to Josh. "He's got to go, Josh!"

"I know." Josh shrugged. "But how?"

How? Magnolia bit her lip. There had to be an answer. They couldn't let their parents *totally* take over their lives. "I know! Josh, you can go to the chess tournament in his place!"

"Me?" Josh's eyes bugged out. "What are you, crazy? I don't know the first thing about playing chess!"

"But Josh, you've got to. Wang can't miss the practice! He's a natural. And, come on, look how much he hates chess. Besides, you're the president!"

"It's true," Wang added from his spot on the floor. "I *really* hate chess."

Josh looked away from them and started pacing in a circle.

"How can I go to the chess tournament? I'll look stupid. I'll lose every single game!"

"That's okay," said Wang. "I lose every game."

"Besides," added Magnolia, "didn't Wang help you lose the election? He even went to the principal's office for it! You owe him one, Josh."

Josh looked down at Wang. Wang lifted his head and stared back at Josh. He looked like a prisoner who sees a ray of light penetrate his gloomy jail cell.

"Would you go for me, Josh? Would you really?" Wang said.

"Of course he'll go," said Magnolia. After all, he *had* to. It was heartbreaking to see Wang slumped on the floor like that, while the other Capulets practiced their sword-fighting all around him.

"You'll go, right, Josh?" she said.

Josh hesitated a second longer. Then he reached down a hand and pulled Wang to his feet.

"Okay, guys," he said. "I'll go."

FIVE

STRATEGIC ALGORITHMS

The bell tinkled as Wang pushed open the door to his parents' grocery shop.

"This is our store," he said to Josh.

"Cool," said Josh, stepping in behind him.

The familiar smell of the grocery store hit Wang as he entered. It smelled of incense, which burned by the statue of the Buddha behind the checkout counter. It smelled of rice in burlap sacks and fresh greens that arrived in waxy cardboard boxes. When he was a little kid, Wang had liked the smell because it felt comfy and familiar—it smelled like home. But nowadays the very hominess of the smell bugged him. It reminded him that he was back again in the same boring old grocery store after school, and not out in the wide world, having adventures.

Oh, well. At least something interesting was finally happening at school, Wang thought. The play was cool, and Josh's new club was awesome. The name was a bit of a problem though: Dunces Anonymous. They should have called themselves something more powerful, like the Parent Avengers. Three young crusaders avenging the wrongs of parents against kids! That was more like it. Maybe he'd suggest it at the next meeting.

In the meantime, though, the important thing was that Josh was helping him get out of playing in the chess tournament. That was the reason he'd invited Josh over this afternoon: they had some important preparation to do.

Wang waved to his mom, who was helping a customer at the checkout counter. Then he led Josh through a grocery aisle toward the back of the store. The aisle was filled with all kinds of stuff you couldn't find in an ordinary supermarket. There were canned quail eggs and pickled lotus stocks, jars of bean-curd paste and salted duck eggs. There were whole rows filled with of different kinds of noodles: the broad, flat, yellow ones; the dry, crunchy ones you could eat right out of the package; the glassy ones spun into long threads; and the squiggly ones pressed into rectangles that came apart when you boiled them.

"Cool," said Josh again, under his breath.

"It's not so cool when you have to spend your Saturday afternoon stocking the shelves," said Wang. "Come on!"

In the stockroom at the back of the store, Wang found his dad unpacking a box of canned water chestnuts.

"Dad, this is my friend, Josh. He wants to learn chess. Can you teach him?"

"Learning new skills is a good thing," his dad replied. "It broadens the mind."

I'd learn new skills if you'd let me stop playing chess, Wang thought. But he didn't say it. Instead, he said, "So, can you teach him, Dad?"

His dad nodded. "I am not a master," he said to Josh, "but I can show you where to begin."

"Great! We'll wait for you upstairs, Dad." Wang grabbed Josh by the arm and dragged him to the checkout counter, where his parents kept shelves of Kung Fu videos to rent out. His mom was busy ringing through customers, so he squeezed behind her and picked out one of his favorites. Josh wouldn't understand the words since it was all in Chinese, but that didn't matter. The important stuff was the action.

"We can watch it after our chess lesson," he told Josh. Then he corrected himself, grinning. "After *your* chess lesson, I should say."

"If I survive it," said Josh.

"Don't worry," said Wang. "You can't be worse than me."

Wang led Josh up a back stairway that went to the apartment above the shop, where he lived with his mom and dad and his two brothers.

In the living room, the chessboard was already set up on a small table in one corner, with two chairs pulled up to it, facing each other. Wang flopped down on the sofa, and Josh sat beside him, casting a nervous eye at the chessboard.

"What if this plan doesn't work?" Josh whispered. "What if the people at the tournament figure out I don't know how to play chess?"

"Don't worry, I'm still in the beginner's group," Wang said. "The tournament's at Centennial High School. You know where that is?"

Josh nodded. "It's near Magnolia's place. She's coming along."

"Good," said Wang.

"But what about your parents? Aren't they going to be there?"

"Naw," said Wang. "They've gotta work in the store. Saturday's our busiest day. But Dad always checks the results on the website."

"Oh, great!" Josh groaned.

"Here," Wang said. "Take this."

He dug into his schoolbag and pulled out a thick paperback book that his dad had given him, entitled *Strategic Algorithms: Learning the Chess Secrets of the Masters*. The book was filled with diagrams of chessboards, followed by lists of mysterious directions that said things like this:

1. e4 e5
2. Nf3 d6
3. Bc4 Bg4
4. Nc3 Nc6
5. o-o Nd4

Wang handed it over and watched Josh's face scrunch up as he tried to read it.

"I don't get it."

"Neither do I. That doesn't matter," Wang said. "Take it to the tournament. It'll make you look like you fit in. It's part of your disguise."

Impersonation and disguise. Schemes and subterfuge.

Finally something exciting was going to happen at a chess tournament. Wang almost felt sorry that he wasn't going to be there to enjoy it.

Josh was stowing the book in his backpack when Wang's dad came upstairs. He motioned Josh to a seat at the chess table, and when they were settled, he picked up the white king and launched into the explanation that Wang had already heard a million times.

"The game of chess is a game of war," Wang's dad said. "You must capture your opponent's king while protecting your own. If you lose your king, you lose the game. The other chess pieces form an army to protect the king…"

Like most other things about the game of chess, his dad's explanation didn't make any sense to Wang. Chess was nothing like a war. There were no guns, no sword-fighting, no hand-to-hand combat. No one ever drew a weapon against his opponent and shouted, "Have at thee, coward!" In chess, no one ever disarmed his opponent with a single twist of his sword or pinned him to the ground until he begged for mercy. That was the stuff Wang wanted to learn at the fencing class on Saturday. He could already picture himself shouting, "*En garde!*" and advancing on his opponent with lightning-fast thrusts and blows.

Wang came out of his daydream just as his dad was putting Josh in checkmate.

"Hey!" said Josh. "I didn't even see that coming."

"You must think three moves ahead. Know the mind of your opponent," Wang's dad said. "Let's play again."

Josh stared glumly at the chessboard. It was obvious he didn't want to play again. Wang knew the feeling.

"What's the point? I'll only lose," Josh mumbled.

"If you lose, it is good. If you win, I have nothing to teach you."

"But I want to win!" Josh protested.

"Then practice," said Wang's dad, handing Josh's captured king back to him. "And learn."

SIX

JOSH IN CHECK

The front steps of Centennial High School swarmed with students arriving for the chess tournament. Josh stood to one side and waited in the cool October air until Magnolia showed up. There was no way he was going in there alone.

Inside, the main hall was hot, filled with people and noisy conversation. Kids of all ages were there. There were teenagers towering over their mothers, and little kids who looked like they should still be learning the alphabet, clasping their daddies' hands. Against the far wall stood a registration table, and taped above the table was a sign.

Welcome to the Centennial Fall Chess Tournament.
The BIGGEST Student Chess Competition in the City!

"Thanks for telling me *that*, Wang," Josh muttered.

"Don't worry," said Magnolia. "It's going to be fine."

Two women sat at the registration table with stacks of paper and boxes of index cards in front of them. In the middle of the crowd, two lines of kids faced the table. Josh noticed that as each kid arrived at the front of the line, one of the women gave the kid a name tag and a folder full of papers. A lot of the parents were scowling over the papers and some were even arguing with the tournament officials, who were standing in one corner of the hall with clipboards and red badges.

"What're they fighting about?" Josh whispered. Magnolia shrugged. How could they be arguing when the tournament hadn't even begun? Maybe that was what Mr. Xiu meant about thinking three moves ahead. Great. He'd just shown up and already he was two moves behind.

If only he'd read *Strategic Algorithms*! Josh fingered the book that was sticking out of his jacket pocket. No matter how hard he'd tried, it hadn't made any sense to him. Instead, he'd taken a beginner's chess book out of the library, and he'd been playing games online all week. Hopefully, it was enough for him to bluff his way through. He still felt nervous about joining one of the lines that was moving, slowly but surely, toward the registration table. Once he registered, there was no turning back.

"Here's the sign-up, Josh," said Magnolia, grabbing his arm and yanking him to the shorter of the two lines. "I'm going to look around a bit," she added.

"Hey, wait…" But before Josh could finish his sentence, Magnolia had disappeared into the crowd.

Most of the kids in Josh's lineup looked kind of geeky, with pale faces and bad haircuts, but in the other registration line, standing right opposite Josh, was a friendly-looking Asian girl about his age. She had a copy of *Chess for Dummies* sticking out of a bag slung over her shoulder, and she smiled at him as he took his place in line. Josh smiled back. At least she didn't look like she thought her brain was three times bigger than everyone else's.

They were almost at the registration table by the time Josh worked up his nerve to talk to her.

"Want to trade books?" said Josh, taking *Strategic Algorithms* out of his pocket.

The girl laughed.

"It's my first tournament," she said.

Me too, Josh wanted to say, but that would have blown his cover. Instead he said, "Good luck."

"Thanks," she said. She looked like she would have said more, but her line moved forward, and it was time for her to step up to the registration table.

Josh watched as one of the registration women asked her name.

"Annie MacGregor," said the girl.

The woman picked up a ruler and crossed Annie's name off on a list. Then she dug into a filing box and pulled out a name tag. Annie was just pinning it on when Josh stepped to the front of his line.

"Name?" said the other woman.

"Jo...uh, Wang Xiu," said Josh.

"I beg your pardon?" The woman looked at him sharply.

At that moment, Josh realized the glaring flaw in the Dunces Anonymous plan. The flaw they should have seen right from the beginning, if only Wang hadn't been so excited about learning sword-fighting, and if only Josh hadn't been so worried about figuring out how to play chess. Anyone with eyes could see that Josh Johnson did not look at all like a Wang Xiu.

Josh looked around frantically for Magnolia. She was nowhere to be seen. He grasped his *Strategic*

Algorithms book, as if it might contain some last-minute strategy to save him. He looked over at Annie, who had paused while pinning on her name tag. If I don't look like a Wang Xiu, he thought, she doesn't look much like an Annie MacGregor either.

He swallowed hard and turned back to the woman. "I'm…I'm adopted."

"You're what?" The woman pinned him with a skeptical eye.

"A-adopted," Josh croaked.

"So am I," said Annie MacGregor. She smiled at him again.

The two registration women looked at each other. Then they looked at the name tags. Then they looked back at Josh and Annie. Then they looked at each other again. One of them shrugged. "Well," she said, "that's life these days."

The other woman shook her head. "You never can tell, I suppose," she muttered, as she fished in the filing box and handed Josh a registration package and a name tag that said *Wang Xiu*.

"Good luck." Annie smiled at him as she turned to go.

"Maybe I'll see you around," Josh said. Then he set off through the crowd to find Magnolia.

He finally found her in the gymnasium, where rows and rows of desks and chairs had been set up, one chessboard on each desk. A chart, taped to the wall, showed which kids played at which desk and at what time. A swarm of kids and parents crowded around the chart.

"Don't worry." Magnolia pulled him away from the crowd. "I already wrote everything down for you. Your first game is at table twenty-six. You're playing a kid called Sean Lu. There're three more games in the day, and at the end of the tournament, everyone gets ranked according to how many games they win or lose, get it?"

"Why don't they rank me at the bottom right now and get it over with?" muttered Josh. Magnolia shushed him and dragged him through the rows to table 26, where Sean Lu greeted him with a distracted handshake. He was already completely focused on the chessboard and the game ahead.

Josh lost his first two matches, but surprisingly, he didn't mind. In fact, he actually found himself enjoying the games. The other players in the beginners' category weren't too much better than he was. He thought he made a few good plays, and sometimes he was even able to anticipate his opponent's moves. But the best thing was the quiet. Nobody had to talk to anybody else.

Nobody bossed anybody else around. Everyone just sat there and played. It was very peaceful.

After the second game he had lunch with Magnolia in the cafeteria and told her about his close call at the registration table. Then they went back up to the gym to check the schedule for the next game. Josh was hoping he might play against Annie MacGregor, but no such luck.

"Look at this." Magnolia snickered. "You're playing a kid called Wilmot Binkle at table nineteen."

"Hmm," Josh said as they made their way to the table. He didn't think it was very nice to snicker at other kids' names, especially since his own name tag said *Wang Xiu*.

Wilmot Binkle was a sweaty kid. That was the first thing Josh noticed. Beads of sweat trickled down his forehead. Sweat soaked the underarms of his *Math Camp* T-shirt. And when Josh shook his hand, it felt like he was squeezing out a damp, sweaty sponge.

Behind Wilmot stood his dad, a tall straight-backed man with a pointy little beard and eyes like a hungry lizard. He scowled at Josh. Josh hoped that Magnolia, who was standing behind him, was scowling right back.

"Good luck," Josh whispered to Wilmot Binkle as they sat down to play. The kid shot him a look of despair. Then the match began.

Josh didn't know much about chess, but even he could tell that Wilmot Binkle wasn't very good. To make matters worse, every time the poor kid lifted his hand to move a piece, his dad would cough or clear his throat or shuffle his feet. Then Wilmot would glance up at him, sweatily, trying to figure out what Mr. Binkle wanted him to do.

Josh played a steady game, using the simple strategies he'd learned from his beginners' chess book. He captured the opposing rook and both knights. Then Wilmot made a mistake and left his queen straight in the path of Josh's bishop. Feeling both excited and guilty, Josh captured the queen. Five moves later, he put Wilmot's king in checkmate.

"Good game," said Josh, extending his hand for Wilmot to shake. Wilmot reached his hand out, smiling, but the boy's dad interrupted.

"Tell me," said Mr. Binkle, pinning Josh with his lizardy eyes. "How did you get a name like Wang Xiu?"

Josh, caught off guard, raised a fumbling hand to his name tag.

"I...I was adopted," Josh squeaked. He twisted around and looked at Magnolia. She stepped forward to stand beside him.

"A likely story!" Mr. Binkle growled.

"Dad, please," pleaded Wilmot. He shot an apologetic glance at Josh and tugged at his father's shirtsleeve. But Mr. Binkle was already waving his arm at a tournament official, who began to make his way toward their table through the rows of kids, many still intent on their chess games.

"What seems to be the problem?" said the official, arriving on the scene. He was a wooly-haired old man wearing a baggy suit and thick glasses, and he carried a sheaf of papers on a clipboard.

"This boy, who just beat my son, claims to be Wang Xiu." Mr. Binkle pointed an accusing finger at Josh. "It's obviously a case of fraudulent impersonation."

"I…I…," Josh began, but he found himself, like Wilmot, breaking into a sweat under Mr. Binkle's stare.

"He's adopted!" Magnolia broke in, taking another step forward.

"And who are you?" Mr. Binkle demanded.

"I'm his twin sister," said Magnolia. "Ping Xiu."

"Oh, this is getting more and more unbelievable!" Mr. Binkle threw his arms in the air.

Magnolia ignored him. She turned toward the tournament official and let out a deep, dramatic sigh.

"You see, sir, our mother was a Canadian missionary in China," Magnolia began in a heartrending voice.

"She was young and innocent when she fell in love with an Australian missionary doctor. But he abandoned her when she got pregnant and left her to face the cruel world all alone. Fearing her condition would bring shame on the whole mission, the nuns forced her to leave. But luckily, she had made friends with some poor rice farmers, the Xius, who were unable to have children of their own! She died in childbirth on the floor of their hut, and they adopted us—her twin babies—giving us the names they had yearned to give their own son and daughter. By good fortune, a kind priest had given my mother a pair of golden candlesticks before she left. Our new parents sold them to pay for a smuggler to take us all to Canada, where we were accepted as refugees, thanks to the letter that my mother had written on her deathbed, explaining the entire story."

Having finished her tragic recital, Magnolia burst into tears. Josh stared at her in astonishment.

"There, there," said the tournament official, patting her on the head.

"Oh, for crying out loud!" raged Mr. Binkle.

"Dad, please," begged Wilmot. Beads of sweat were running down his face and trickling under the collar of his T-shirt.

"Really, Mr. Binkle, haven't these poor orphans suffered enough hardships already?" said the tournament official sternly. "As far as I'm concerned, young Wang here has won the match fair and square."

"Oh, thank you, sir!" exclaimed Magnolia, turning a pair of adoring eyes on him.

Mr. Binkle grabbed his son by the hand and shot a look of disgust at everyone around him.

"You haven't heard the last of this!" he cried. "I'm taking this to the board of directors!"

Mr. Binkle marched off through the rows of desks, dragging Wilmot behind him. But Josh folded his hands together and bowed very low to the tournament official, in what he imagined to be a Chinese gesture of gratitude.

"Holy cow, Magnolia, are you sure you want to quit the school play?" Josh said, as they walked home after the chess tournament. They were sharing a bag of chips that Josh had bought at the corner store near the school.

Magnolia took a potato chip out of the bag and rolled her eyes.

"I thought you were on my side, Josh."

"I am, but, wow! You were great back there! I mean, you're a really good actress."

"That was different. That was fun. But playing Juliet with Emmett Blackwell..."

"I know, it's pretty disgusting." Josh munched on a chip. "Still, at least you're good at it. I wish I was *that* good at something."

"What are you talking about?" Magnolia stopped in her tracks and turned to look at him. "You're a good president!"

"No, I'm not." Josh scuffed some dead leaves on the sidewalk with the toe of his sneaker.

"Sure you are. Presidents are supposed to help people, aren't they?" Magnolia continued. "And you just helped Wang by going to the chess tournament in his place, didn't you? Even though you could have gotten in trouble for it."

Josh shrugged. "I guess."

"Well then, that just proves that you're a good president! Besides," she added, "you started Dunces Anonymous, and it's the coolest club in the school."

Josh didn't say anything, and they started walking again, eating their chips. But her words stayed in his head after he left her at her house, and all the way home. When he got to the lobby of his mom's condo building, he didn't take his usual route up the back stairs. Instead he stood right there, next to two adults he didn't know, waiting for the shiny gold elevator doors to open. He rode with them all the way up to the sixth floor. If they ask me who I am, he thought, I'll just tell them I'm the president. The president of the coolest club in the school.

SEVEN

OPERATION FREE JULIET

Emmett Blackwell was really getting on Magnolia's nerves. He wouldn't even speak to her when she was just Schoolgirl Number Three, and now that she was Juliet, he wouldn't lay off. Planning to kiss her on performance night! Calling her "my Juliet" in the schoolyard and winking at her at recess! It was gross!

She looked down on him from the wooden platform that was supposed to represent Juliet's balcony. It was six weeks until performance night and they were practicing the balcony scene—again. Magnolia wished they would rehearse Act Five instead, where Juliet commits suicide. It was the only part of the play that Magnolia found satisfying.

Now, as Emmett stood below her on the stage, vowing his undying love, Magnolia felt an urge to pour boiling oil on him, the way old-time knights did when enemies tried to scale their battlements. Magnolia glanced at her mother, who was sitting on her usual chair facing center stage. Mom would not be impressed if Magnolia poured boiling oil on Romeo.

She looked down again at Emmett, who was gazing up at her, love struck.

"'See! How she leans her cheek upon her hand!'" Emmett exclaimed. "'Oh, that I were a glove upon that hand, that I might touch that cheek!'"

That was Magnolia's cue. She stepped forward.

"'O, Romeo, Romeo, wherefore art thou...'"

"Hold it! Stop! Stop!" shouted Mrs. Karloff, walking out onto the stage. "Juliet, darling, it's nighttime. It's dark outside. You walk out onto your balcony. You are carrying...what?"

"A lantern," Magnolia grumbled.

"Right. So where is it?"

"I couldn't find it." Backstage was a mess, as usual. The props table, which had started out fairly neat, was now completely covered in a heap of plastic swords from the Capulets and the Montagues. The other props were scattered in and around the swords at random, along with a jumble of things that people had left there after using the gymnasium and which had nothing whatsoever to do with the play: pairs of smelly gym shorts, lost textbooks, orphan running shoes.

"Go and look for the lantern, darling," sighed Mrs. Karloff. "If you don't practice with it now, you'll fumble it during the performance." Mrs. Karloff clapped her hands. "All right, everyone. Take five."

Magnolia clumped down the steps at the back of the platform, holding up the long cotton skirt that Mrs. Karloff made her wear for rehearsals. On performance night, she would be wearing a floor-length princess dress. Mrs. Karloff called it "romantic."

"Romantic!" Magnolia harrumphed, nearly tripping over the skirt. "What's so romantic about a dress you can't even walk in?"

"Oh, Magnolia! I found the lantern!" Hannah Flynn came running up to her, holding a battered camping light.

"Thanks," said Magnolia, taking it.

"Oh, Magnolia!" Hannah continued breathlessly. "Is it really true that you're Emmett's *girlfriend*?"

"Where did you hear *that*?"

"It's on the *Rapsheet*. I saw it this morning! I thought I was going to die!"

The *Rapsheet*. That figured. The *Rapsheet*— www.rapsheet.org—was the most popular student blog at Oakview Public School. It was part school news, part school sports and mostly school gossip. Magnolia didn't know who ran the *Rapsheet*, but she strongly suspected that this little piece of "information" had been passed on to whoever-it-was by Emmett himself.

"Well, it's not true," said Magnolia. "Emmett and I have a purely *professional* relationship."

"That's what *you* say. That's not what everyone else says." Hannah giggled. "Isn't he cute? Doesn't it make you want to die when he calls you 'my heart's dear love'?"

"No," said Magnolia. Actually, it made her want to puke.

"Emmett Blackwell's girlfriend!" Hannah sighed.

"I'm not his girlfriend!" Magnolia shouted. Why couldn't Hannah get that through her dorky head?

"Places everyone!" Mrs. Karloff clapped her hands.

Magnolia looked out onstage, where Emmett lurked in wait for her.

"'What light through yonder window breaks? It is the east, and Juliet is the sun!'" Emmett proclaimed.

Maybe, Magnolia thought, jumping off a roof wasn't such a bad idea, after all.

After rehearsal, Magnolia called an emergency meeting of Dunces Anonymous at the jungle gym in the schoolyard.

"I've got to get out of this, you guys," she said to Josh and Wang, after filling them in on Emmett's escalating romantic intentions. An October wind brushed the back of her neck, and she pulled her jean jacket tighter around her.

"I know!" said Wang, jumping up to swing on the monkey bars. "What if one of us pulls the fire alarm on performance night?"

The idea was tempting.

"We'd get in trouble if we got caught…," Magnolia hesitated.

"And it would ruin the play for everyone else, which wouldn't be fair," said Josh.

"Yeah, I guess you're right," Wang admitted. "And the fight scenes are going to be really cool."

"Lucky you, you don't have to kiss anyone," Magnolia grumbled.

Josh swung slowly on the swing, dragging his feet through a pile of dead leaves that had fallen from the big maple tree in the corner of the schoolyard. Wang jumped down from the monkey bars.

"Maybe you should just quit. Tell your mom you're not going to do it!" Wang said.

"Are you nuts?" Magnolia said. "She'll have a total meltdown. First she'll cry. Then she'll say, 'Playing Juliet was my lifelong dream! Now you have the chance, and you're throwing it away!' Then she'll make me feel like I'm ruining her life all over again."

Magnolia crossed her arms.

"I can't do it," she said. "I'd rather get kissed by Emmett Blackwell."

Wang jumped back onto the monkey bars. Josh spun the swing clockwise until the chains were twisted together; then he dangled his legs in the pile of leaves while the swing slowly unwound.

"Mr. Xiu says, 'Know the mind of your opponent,'" Josh reflected. "What do we know about your mom, Magnolia?"

"Well, she loves acting—movies, TV, the stage, it doesn't matter. She says she loves being swept up in the drama," Magnolia began. "And, of course, she believes in True Love. Like that soap opera she watches.

It doesn't matter how ridiculous the plot is, if it's about True Love, she'll fall for it."

"True Love," Josh repeated, scuffling his sneakers through the leaves. "So if we could convince her that Emmett had found the One True Love of His Life, she'd want them to be together, no matter what?"

"Yeah, of course," said Magnolia.

"Even if it wasn't you?"

"Yeah, as long as it was the Love of His Life."

"Then I think I've got a plan," said Josh. "We'll call it Operation Free Juliet."

EIGHT

ROSES FOR EMMETT

Josh's plan for Operation Free Juliet required cunning and courage. Naturally, Wang had volunteered for the mission. "Cunning is my middle name," he'd told Josh. Now it was time for him to live up to his bold words.

It was Wednesday afternoon at four o'clock. Onstage, the rehearsal was in full swing. They were practicing the scene between Romeo and the priest. Josh stood at his post beside the curtain pull-cord. Around the gym, the other actors were doing homework or memorizing their lines, waiting for their turn to come onstage. Some had gone out to the corner store to stock up on snacks. No one would miss Wang if he snuck out for a few minutes.

Stealthily, Wang pushed open the door to the boys' change room. The coast was clear. Moving quickly, he opened his backpack and took out a dozen roses that Magnolia had salvaged from her cousin's wedding that past weekend. Emmett's backpack with the *Anne of Green Gables* logo on the front pocket was sitting on a bench. Swiftly, Wang opened the backpack and placed the roses inside, arranging them so that the blooms stuck out of the top and sent a girly perfume wafting over the change room's usual smell of stinky socks and old gym shoes. He tucked a pink note amid the flowers. Then he retreated to the gym and waited for the end of rehearsal.

As Wang had expected, the flowers were the first thing the boys noticed when they crowded into the change room at 5:00 PM. Wang and Josh brought up the rear of the crowd, sliding quietly onto a bench in the far corner to watch the action unfold.

"Hey! There's a note!" shouted Declan, the red-headed, cat-faced boy who played Juliet's cousin, Tybalt. He pounced on the backpack and grabbed the folded pink notepaper before Emmett could stop him. Then he jumped up on a bench, and read aloud in a mocking tone:

I sit and watch you every day
And wish I knew the words to say.

I'm too afraid to let you know
I wish you were my Romeo.

—A Secret Admirer"

"Emmett's got a secret admirer!" someone shouted. Catcalls erupted from all corners of the change room.

Emmett looked down his nose. "All great actors have secret admirers."

He snatched the note back from Declan. Then he plucked a rose from the bouquet, held it to his nose and sniffed it loudly.

"Ahh! 'A rose by any other name would smell as sweet!'" he exclaimed. He swung his backpack onto his shoulder, raised his chin in the air and marched out the door.

The boys broke into laughter and jeers, but Wang looked at Josh and grinned. Operation Free Juliet had begun.

Two days later, Wang snuck into Emmett's class at recess and left a package of candy hearts on his desk. The following week, he wrote a poem in chalk on the blackboard of Emmett's classroom at lunch hour:

Lovely Emmett, tall and fine,
Oh, how I wish that you were mine!

Very handsome, eyes so blue,
Emmett Blackwell, I love you!

—*A Secret Admirer*

The school was abuzz, trying to guess the identity of the Secret Admirer. The *Rapsheet* had started an online poll where kids could vote for their favorite suspect. But Dunces Anonymous had even greater schemes to make Emmett believe that someone at school was his One True Love.

"You ready for this?" Josh whispered to Wang the next day, as they hid in a back stairwell at the end of the second-floor hallway near Emmett's locker. There was no rehearsal that day; the gym was being used for volleyball practice. The end-of-school bell had just rung, and though the hall was filled with kids jostling to get out of school, the stairwell itself was empty. That was because at the bottom of the stairs there was a heavy door with a notice affixed to it: *Emergency Exit Only. Alarm Will Sound If Door Opened.*

"Are you sure of the combination?" Wang whispered back.

"I told you: nineteen, thirty-five, fifty-one," said Josh. "Look."

Josh pulled his cell phone out of his pocket. He pushed a button on the phone and a video appeared of Emmett's hand, turning the combination lock from his school locker.

"How'd you get that?" Wang hissed.

"Magnolia got it. She went to talk to Emmett at lunch hour. She said it nearly killed her to stand that close to him!"

"Awesome!" Wang whispered. "Let's check our supplies." Wang opened his backpack, and the two of them looked inside. A powder blue stuffed teddy bear that Wang had bought from a dollar-store remainder bin sat there with a note pinned at its heart:

Roses are red,
Poems are clever,
Kiss me once
And I'm yours forever!

       —A Secret Admirer

"Okay," whispered Josh. "Let's do this."

The noise in the hallway had died down. Josh opened the stairwell door a crack, and he and Wang peered out. The hall was empty. Emmett's locker was about ten steps away. Twenty steps beyond that, the hallway turned a corner, leading to more classrooms.

"The coast is clear!" said Josh. "I'll stand guard at the corner. If I see anyone coming, I'll shout and you run for cover."

Wang nodded. They clasped hands once for luck and split up to carry out the mission.

Wang tiptoed to Emmett's locker. He'd memorized the combination, but his fingers were shaking as he reached for the lock. They could get into real trouble for breaking into someone's locker! Be brave, he told himself. Operation Free Juliet must not fail.

He grasped the lock, dialed the combination, yanked and felt the bolt yield. Carefully, he opened the locker door.

Emmett's locker was as neat as a girl's bedroom. All his school books lay stacked on the shelf above the coat hooks, with a paperback copy of *Romeo and Juliet* at the very top of the stack. On the door of the locker hung a square mirror with a comb tucked behind it. Below the mirror was a photograph of Emmett with the cast of the *Anne of Green Gables* television series. Above the mirror, Emmett had taped the love notes from his Secret Admirer.

Wang reached into his backpack and pulled out the stuffed teddy bear. Where to put it? On the floor of the locker, he decided, with Emmett's copy of *Romeo and Juliet* tucked between its paws. He set the teddy bear down and was reaching for the book at the top of the pile when he heard Josh's voice saying, very loudly, "Hey, Emmett! Wow! It's great to bump into you!"

Wang jumped. The stack of books toppled from the locker shelf onto the hallway floor. Wang flung himself to the ground and started shoveling the books back into the locker, burying the teddy bear under French grammar and math equations.

"Hey wait, Emmett!" Josh's voice sounded desperate. "I saw you in that *Anne of Green Gables* show. You were great. Could you, um, could you give me your autograph?"

Wang threw the last book in, slammed the door, snapped the lock closed, grabbed his backpack and raced down the hallway. Ten steps took him to the back stairwell. He pounded down the stairs and burst through the door at the bottom, ignoring the sign that said *Emergency Exit Only*. An alarm clanged as he sprinted across the teachers' parking lot. He ran for his life, never looking back, and didn't stop running until he reached his parents' grocery store, which was one bridge, two parks and seven bus stops away.

On the sidewalk outside the store, Wang bent over to catch his breath. He didn't think anyone had seen him running out of the school building. He hoped Josh had gotten away without arousing any suspicions. When his heart stopped thumping and his breathing returned to normal, Wang climbed the front steps, grabbed the mail from the mailbox and went inside.

His mom was chatting with a customer at the checkout. Farther back, in the produce section, his dad was discussing the freshness of the bok choy with another customer. Wang said "Hi" in what he hoped was a casual manner; then he quickly climbed the stairs to the apartment where his two brothers were sitting on the sofa, playing video games. He was about to drop the mail on the hall table when the letter on the top of the pile caught his eye. It was addressed to Wang Xiu and his father, Mr. Ham Xiu, and it was from the National Organization of Public School Chess Associations. Wang, still on the alert from his break-and-enter mission, felt his heart start to pound again like the drum of an enemy army, warning of danger.

Wang glanced around. His brothers were glued to their video game. There was no sign of his parents. Quickly, he slipped the letter into his jacket pocket. Then he tiptoed to his room and shut the door.

Using a trick he'd seen in a movie, Wang wedged a chair underneath the doorknob to stop anyone from coming in. Then he pulled the letter out of his bag and looked at it again. The National Organization of Public School Chess Associations. It looked official. It looked like trouble.

His heart raced. His fingers crept around the envelope flap. He knew he shouldn't open the letter without his dad. But on the other hand, good guys sometimes did a lot worse things than opening other people's letters. They broke into safes and wrecked cars and even killed their enemies. The kung-fu movies his parents rented out to customers were filled with furniture getting splintered to bits and motorcycle chases through crowded markets, where whole stalls full of fresh vegetables were overturned and went to waste. Compared to that, Wang wasn't doing anything really bad. If it was just an innocent letter, he could always show it to his dad afterward. And if it was trouble... Well, if it was trouble, he didn't dare let his dad find out about it. He had no choice. "Sorry, Dad," Wang whispered as he ripped the letter open.

Dear Mr. Xiu and Wang,

We regret to inform you that a formal complaint has been lodged against Wang, by Mr. Conrad Binkle and his son, Wilmot Binkle.

The Binkles accuse Wang of sending another student to take his place at the recent Centennial High School Fall Chess Tournament in order to improve his chess ranking.

As you can understand, the National Organization of Public School Chess Associations takes all allegations of fraudulent impersonation extremely seriously. It is not acceptable for a student to claim false victories by sending another student to play in his place.

We have decided to deal with this complaint at our Annual General Meeting on November 20. We invite you both to attend the meeting and answer the allegations.

If the complaint proves to be true, we regret to inform you that Wang will be expelled from his school chess club and banned from competition in all Public School chess tournaments.

Sincerely yours,
The Board of Directors
National Organization of Public School Chess Associations

Wang dropped the letter on his bed. His fingers trembled. His stomach burned like he'd swallowed a bottle of hot vinegar. *Fraudulent impersonation?* Sending another player to improve his chess ranking?

"It wasn't like that at all!" he moaned. But who was going to believe him? Why hadn't he just told his dad in the first place that he wanted to go to fencing practice instead of the chess tournament? Now it was too late. Now he'd be expelled from the chess club in disgrace, and every time the father of another chess player came into the store, his dad would have to hang his head in shame.

Wang sank to the bed. There had to be some way out of this. He looked at the letter again. The board of directors' meeting was on November 20. Less than three weeks away. Less than three weeks to come up with a plan. Taking a deep breath, he grabbed the letter and stuffed it to the very bottom of his backpack. Then he slipped the chair out from under the door handle and snuck through the back hallway to the kitchen. There was no one around. Through the wall, he could hear the beeps and shouts of his brothers playing video games in the living room. Stealthily, Wang picked up the phone and dialed Josh.

"Hey, Prez," he said. "We've got a problem."

NINE

YOUNG LEADERS
OF THE FUTURE

"So, how's my favorite Young Leader of the Future?" Josh's mom asked as they sat down to dinner a few days later.

"Fine," said Josh. Actually, he wasn't fine at all. He had a lot on his mind. The day after the locker break-in, the principal had announced that if the person who set off the school's fire alarm was caught, he'd be suspended for a week. Operation Free Juliet still wasn't finished. And now, they had to come up with a plan to thwart the Binkles.

All this plotting and planning was making Josh's brain hurt. It was like trying to play three chess matches at once.

Josh had been playing a lot of chess online since the tournament. He enjoyed the strategy and the idea of thinking three moves ahead of your opponent. It wasn't easy, but it was a lot less complicated than real life. In chess, people had to follow rules about where and when they could move their pieces. In real life, people seemed to do things without following any rules at all. And in chess, if you lost, you could set up the pieces and start over again. In real life, you didn't get to go back to the beginning and start over, as though your mistakes had never happened. In real life, when things went wrong, real people could get into real trouble. The idea of him and his friends getting into trouble weighed heavily on Josh's mind.

To top it all off, Mom had made something weird for dinner again. It was supposed to be lasagna, but Josh had his doubts about that. He rooted around at it with his fork, searching for something lasagna-like: a hunk of tomato or a piece of hamburger meat. No luck. Even the noodles didn't look like regular noodles. They were green, with strange vegetables like leeks and artichokes sandwiched between them, all smothered in a white, gooey sauce. On top, like a birthday candle stuck in a piece of cake, was something that looked like a tiny twig. It still had leaves on it, whatever it was. Josh flicked it off with his fork. He didn't eat twigs.

"So what have you kids been doing?" his mother asked, pouring herself a glass of wine.

"Huh?" said Josh.

"In the club."

"Oh," said Josh, taking an experimental bite of his dinner. "Well, we've got one guy who's competing in chess tournaments and a girl who has the lead role in the school play."

And we're trying to get both of them out of it, he thought. But of course, he didn't tell his mom that.

"That's wonderful," said his mother. "And what about you?"

"I'm the president," said Josh. That seemed pretty obvious.

"Yes, but what have you done?" said his mother.

Josh stopped puzzling over his food and started puzzling over his mother instead. It seemed she was never happy unless he was trying to "better himself." But what was better than president? Wasn't president the best you could be?

"I'm the president," Josh repeated.

"Yes, honey, but presidents have to *do* things," she said. "Like organize debating tournaments or mock parliaments or entrepreneurship seminars."

Josh thought about that, biting into a piece of green noodle. He wondered if he could tell his mom about any of the things he'd done as president of Dunces Anonymous. Impersonating Wang at a chess tournament? Nope. Writing fake love poems to Emmett Blackwell? Nope. Helping Wang break into Emmett's locker? Double nope. Josh sighed. Once again, it seemed there was nothing he could say to his mother that would make her happy.

"You know," his mother continued, digging into her supposedly-lasagna dinner. "I was talking to Stacey Hogarth's mom the other day about your club, and she's sure that Stacey's never heard of it."

"Mom!" Josh wailed. "What were you doing, talking to Stacey Hogarth's mother?"

"I ran into her at a meeting of the Women's Business Council, dear. In any case, your club doesn't seem to have a very high profile at school."

"Of course we don't have a high profile, Mom! There's only three of us in the club!"

"Only three of you?" His mom tapped the tines of her fork against her placemat. "Then it's obvious. You have to hold a membership drive!"

"A membership drive?" said Magnolia, when Josh presented the idea at the next meeting of Dunces Anonymous. "But we don't want any new members!"

"More members mean more problems," Wang agreed. "We already have enough problems as it is. And besides, what are we going to do about the Binkles?"

Josh tapped his little wooden mallet thoughtfully on his desk. Stacey's bake-sale committee had disbanded after the successful Halloween bake sale, and her Christmas party committee didn't start meeting until next week, so they had a rare chance to use the classroom at lunch hour.

"That's not the only thing, guys," said Josh. "My mom thinks...well, I kind of told her...that it's a club for junior achievers. And she thinks it's called Young Leaders of the Future."

"Young Leaders of the Future?" Magnolia winced. "That's lame."

"I was thinking we could call it the Parent Avengers," Wang interjected. "Three young crusaders avenging the wrongs of parents against kids!"

"Why are we changing the name of the club?" Magnolia protested.

"Guys! Guys!" Josh banged the mallet on his desk. "I haven't told you the most important thing yet! Guess who my mom told about the club?"

But before Wang and Magnolia could guess, the classroom door opened and in walked Stacey Hogarth.

Stacey was a tall girl with a snub nose and brown hair pulled back tight in a ponytail. She marched up to Josh and stood in front of him, arms crossed.

"Your mother told my mother that you're the president of a club called Young Leaders of the Future, and I want to join," Stacey said.

"Sorry," said Josh, gripping the mallet for courage. "The club is all full up."

"That's impossible," Stacey replied. "Your mother told my mother that you're having a membership drive."

Josh opened his mouth and closed it again. What was he supposed to say to that?

"That's right," Wang said. "The membership drive was incredibly successful, and now we're all full up. Sorry. Try again next year."

Stacey glared around the room skeptically.

"There's only three of you here," she said.

"That's right," Magnolia answered this time. "Because we're the President's Special Committee."

"That's fine then," said Stacey, plopping her bum down on Josh's desk. "Because I want to be on the President's Special Committee too. I've got lots of ideas for this club!"

Josh looked at Stacey Hogarth's bum on his desk. It was wearing a short black skirt with a pocket on each butt-cheek. He didn't like it there. It made him feel very crowded.

"Stacey," said Josh, trying to mimic his mother's most businesslike tone. "We cannot move forward under these parameters."

"What are you talking about?" Stacey asked. She twisted around to look at him.

"He means," said Magnolia, standing up and crossing her arms, "that you can't join the President's Special Committee without an application letter."

"An application letter?" said Stacey.

"That's right," Wang stood up too. "With a list of all your extracurricular activities."

"All my extracurricular activities?" said Stacey.

"Since kindergarten," Magnolia added.

"And three teachers' signatures!" Wang put in.

"Three teacher's signatures!"

"Right," said Josh, raising his mallet. "As president, I now declare this meeting over!"

"Over? Hey…," Stacey spluttered.

Josh brought down the mallet and whacked it very hard, right next to Stacey Hogarth's bum. He scooted out of his chair and ran to the classroom door, Magnolia and Wang close behind him.

"You can't do this, you guys!" Stacey shouted,

jumping down from the desk. But Josh, Wang and Magnolia were already out the door and into the hallway when they heard her call after them, "You can't stop me from being a Young Leader of the Future!"

TEN

EMMETT MAKES HIS MOVE

A week and a half until the dress rehearsal! Magnolia walked out of the school building, deep in thought. Mrs. Karloff had just finished explaining everything about the dress rehearsal to the cast. It was going to be a big deal. Everyone would be wearing costumes; there would be lights and sound effects and props, sword-fights and sets and a rope ladder for Romeo to climb up to Juliet's balcony.

What Mrs. Karloff didn't know was that the dress rehearsal would also be the scene of the final act in Operation Free Juliet.

Their plan was to make Magnolia's mother believe that Emmett had a secret admirer who was his One True Love—a girl fated to play Juliet opposite Emmett's Romeo. Magnolia would reveal the identity of the secret admirer in a dramatic scene during the dress rehearsal, when her mother, enthralled by the action on stage, would fall for the story. She'd never guess it was all a ruse cooked up by Dunces Anonymous! Magnolia shivered and tucked her hands into the sleeves of her trench coat. It was late afternoon on a cold November day, the last rays of sunlight glinting on the icicles that hung from the eaves of the school building.

For the past two weeks, Magnolia had been thinking of what she would say during the scene of dramatic revelation. Now, as her shoes crunched through the film of ice that had formed on the puddles in the schoolyard, Magnolia practiced the lines in her head. She tried them this way and that, considering when to pause and which words to emphasize for maximum dramatic effect. She was so preoccupied that she didn't notice Emmett until he jumped off of the jungle gym and landed right in front of her.

"'What light through yonder window breaks? It is the east, and Juliet is the sun!'"

"Knock it off, Emmett," Magnolia grumbled, recovering from her surprise. "Rehearsal's over."

She moved to the right to step around him, but Emmett jumped in front of her again.

"I am not rehearsing, my bright angel," he said. He looked at her with love-struck eyes.

"Then stop bugging me," Magnolia answered, irritated. She tried to step around him again, this time to the left, but again Emmett jumped in front of her.

"Not bugging, but begging, my heart's dear love." Emmett grabbed her hand and fell to one knee. "Begging you for one tender kiss!"

"Emmett!" She tried to shake her hand free, but he held it tight. "Stop it! You can't hold hands in the schoolyard! You'll get a detention!"

"Then I will be like Romeo," Emmett exclaimed. "Banished from the sight of my true love!"

A crazy look gleamed in his eye. He pulled her hand toward him. She felt his wet lips on her fingers.

"Emmett!" Magnolia ripped her hand away. She glanced around for an escape route, but the jungle gym blocked her way. She jumped onto the monkey bars, feeling her palms sting as they gripped the cold metal. She swung herself up and climbed to the top platform.

"Behold, fair Juliet upon her balcony!" Emmett shouted from below. "With love's light wings, I come to thee!"

He jumped onto the monkey bars and began to climb up after her. Magnolia looked around. The only way down was the fireman's pole. She leaped onto the ice-cold pole and slid, her trench coat flapping around her legs, until she landed with a thud in the sand. She took off at a run across the schoolyard.

Dashing through the gate that led to the street, Magnolia glanced over her shoulder and saw Emmett standing at the top of the jungle gym, waving his arms madly.

"Do not flee from me, Magnolia!" he shouted after her. "I know you are my Secret Admirer!"

Magnolia burst into the kitchen, panting. Her mother was singing along to a Céline Dion CD and stirring something on the stove. It smelled like curried chicken. At her feet, little Garland was grabbing all the plastic containers out of a drawer and flinging them across the floor.

"That Emmett Blackwell!" Magnolia exclaimed, planting her hands on her hips for dramatic effect.

"What about him, dear?" her mother paused, wooden spoon suspended above the frying pan. "He seems like a lovely boy."

"He wants to kiss me!"

"Well, of course he does, dear. You're his Juliet!" her mom trilled.

"Oh, sheesh!" Magnolia turned and stomped out of the kitchen, ignoring her mother, who was calling after her:

"Do you want to talk about it, dear?"

Not to you, Magnolia thought.

She stomped upstairs and opened the door to her dad's study without knocking. Inside, her dad and her two middle brothers, Randy and Robin, were standing squashed together on a bridge made of Popsicle sticks. Her dad was an engineer, and he'd been helping the boys with their science fair project.

"Magnolia! Just in time!" her dad motioned her to join them on the bridge. "We need another heavy object!"

"Thanks a lot!" Magnolia huffed.

"Sweetheart, I didn't mean…," her dad began, but she was already out the door.

Her family was impossible! There was nothing left to do but call Wang and Josh for an emergency meeting at her house after supper.

"So now Emmett thinks I'm his secret admirer!" Magnolia concluded, after telling the boys the story of her encounter in the schoolyard. She flung herself backward onto the sofa. Luckily, her mom and dad were too busy putting her younger brothers to bed to be curious about their meeting.

"That wasn't supposed to happen," said Wang.

"No kidding," said Magnolia. "It's going to ruin everything!"

"I hate to tell you guys this," said Josh, "but that's not our only problem." He drew a piece of paper from his back pocket.

"Sorry," Josh continued. "I was going to tell you about this at school tomorrow, but since you're here…" He handed the paper to Magnolia. "Stacey Hogarth just dropped this off. It's her application letter to join the club."

Magnolia took the letter from Josh. It was printed on heavy cream-colored stationery with the initials *SH* in fancy type at the top. She unfolded it and read aloud.

"Dear Josh,

I would really like to join the President's Special Committee of Young Leaders of the Future. Here is a list of my Leadership Positions and Extracurricular Activities:

Kindergarten: Circle Time Monitor. Head Blackboard-Eraser Cleaner.

Grade One: Captain of the I Can Read Team. Math Olympics gold medalist.

Grade Two: President of the Junior Careers Club.

Grade Three..."

"The Junior Careers Club?" Wang snatched the letter away from Magnolia before she could finish reading it. "We're doomed!"

Magnolia snatched the letter back.

"No, we're not. It's simple," she said to Josh. "You're the president. Just tell her she's not allowed to join."

"I can't do that." Josh pulled a second piece of paper from his pocket. "Stacey dropped this off too."

Magnolia took it from Josh's hand. It was a photocopy of a page of a book. In the top right-hand corner was written in small type: *Oakview Public School Official Rule Book*. Magnolia skimmed down the page to the lines highlighted in yellow and read aloud.

"*Rule number one hundred and thirteen-b: All school clubs shall be open to all students, regardless of age, gender, religion, race, ethnicity, physical or mental disabilities or socioeconomic status.*"

"What's a socioeconomic status?" said Wang.

"Beats me," said Josh. "Whatever it is, I guess Stacey's got one. But in any case, this rule says we have to let her into the club."

Magnolia turned the paper over in her hands. Then she handed it back to Josh. "Well, what are you going to do about it?"

"Me?" said Josh.

"Of course, you. You're the president, aren't you?" Magnolia demanded.

"Yeah, but…" Josh trailed off.

"I hate to mention this, guys," Wang piped up. "But we also have to figure out what to do about the Binkles."

"Sheesh!" Magnolia flopped backward on to the sofa cushions. "I've never seen a club with so many problems! I bet if Stacey knew how many problems we have, she wouldn't even *want* to join!"

Josh paced over to the window. Then he turned around and looked at Magnolia. "Wait a minute. Say that again."

"I said," Magnolia huffed, "that if Stacey knew how many problems we have, she wouldn't even *want* to join the club."

"That's it!" Josh exclaimed. "All we have to do is convince Stacey that she doesn't really want to join the club!"

"But how?" said Wang.

"Yeah, how?" said Magnolia.

"I've got an idea," said Josh. "A couple of years ago, my mom joined this political party. But she quit because she said there were too many scandals. Maybe we could have, you know, a scandal."

"A scandal!" Magnolia jumped from the sofa. A scandal had dramatic possibilities. Once, in *Young Hearts Afire*, there was a huge scandal when the chief surgeon, Dr. Deirhart, was accused of stealing money from the hospital's charity fund. The scandal only cleared up when the doctor proved that the hospital's chief accountant was the true culprit.

"I know," she said. "Josh could steal all the money from the club's bank account!"

"That's illegal!" Josh protested. "Besides, we don't have a bank account."

"Oh, yeah." Magnolia slumped back onto the sofa.

"Maybe you could beat up a kid in the schoolyard!"

Wang suggested, sketching a few punches in the air.

"Wang! I'm not going to beat up anybody!" Josh looked at Wang like he was crazy.

"Okay, forget that." Wang lowered his fists with some disappointment. A moment later, he perked up again. "I know! How about a l-o-o-o-ve scandal?"

"A love scandal?" said Josh.

"Yeah!" Wang's eyes grew wide. "What if someone caught you two kissing in the schoolyard?"

"Kissing?!" Magnolia threw up her hands in disgust. "How come *I* always have to *kiss* someone?"

"You don't really have to kiss! You just have to look like you're kissing. For the camera."

"The camera?" Josh said doubtfully.

"Sure!" said Wang. "I'll take a picture, and then we'll write something up and send it in to the *Rapsheet*. It'll be great!"

"How do we know they'll put it up on the website?" Magnolia asked.

"No problem. The guy who runs it is a Capulet," said Wang.

"I don't know, you guys," said Josh.

"Well, I think it's a good idea!" said Magnolia. "Besides, it'll prove to Emmett Blackwell that I'm not his Secret Admirer!"

"Come on, Prez! It's a plan that solves two problems at once! What could be better than that?" said Wang.

"Maybe a plan that doesn't make me totally embarrassed," Josh muttered.

"It's only acting," said Magnolia. "It's not for real."

"I know, but…," said Josh.

"Great!" said Wang. "Then we'll meet Saturday morning at seven in the schoolyard!"

ELEVEN

SCANDAL ON THE RAPSHEET

Wang pulled up the *Rapsheet* on his computer and leaned back in his chair. Another cunning plan, flawlessly executed.

Across the top of the screen blared the headline: *LOVE SCANDAL ROCKS YOUNG LEADERS!*

Beneath the headline was the photo that he'd taken in the schoolyard on Saturday morning. The sun was glinting off the frost on the jungle gym, creating a romantic halo effect. Josh and Magnolia were standing on the sand, their faces half hidden by one of the jungle gym's wooden posts. Their hands were clasped together on the post and they were leaning in close to each other. Though you couldn't actually see their lips touching—that part was hidden by the post—it didn't take much to imagine a passionate kiss.

It was a photographic masterpiece! And the story, which Magnolia had helped write, was pretty good too:

Josh Johnson, the president of the Young Leaders of the Future club, was caught breaking school rules today, when an informant for the Rapsheet *snapped this photo of him in the schoolyard kissing another member of the club, Magnolia Montcrieff.*

Magnolia is playing Juliet in the upcoming school play, Romeo and Juliet. *Rumor had it that she was dating the other star of the play, Emmett Blackwell.*

Looks like they're toast!

In fact, our informant tells us that Josh and Magnolia are Going Out.

"They're definitely more than just friends," said our confidential informant. "They're totally into each other!"

Hey, Josh, it's a school club, not a nightclub! Keep your hands to yourself, you girl mauler!

"Girl mauler!" Josh exclaimed, right in Wang's ear. He and Magnolia were reading the blog over Wang's shoulder, on the computer in Wang's living room.

A chopping sound came from the kitchen, where Wang's dad was preparing supper while his mom closed up the store downstairs.

"I thought of that myself," said Wang. "Pretty good, eh?"

"If you want to ruin my reputation!"

"We can't have a scandal without ruining your reputation, Josh," Magnolia pointed out. "I like 'girl mauler.' I bet it'll keep Stacey away."

"Yeah, Josh might maul her! *Grrr!*" Wang clawed the air like a lion. Josh sighed.

"Hopefully it'll convince Emmett that you're not his secret admirer," Josh said, turning to Magnolia.

"So all our problems are solved," Magnolia said.

She sounded so satisfied that Wang couldn't help bursting out, "Not all of them!" He looked toward the kitchen door and lowered his voice. "What about the Binkles?"

He'd tried to be patient, helping Josh and Magnolia with their problems. But now things were getting desperate. The board of directors' meeting was coming up quickly.

"If we don't think of something, I'm going to get kicked out of the chess club!"

"I thought you didn't want to be in the chess club anyway," said Magnolia.

"Yeah, but I can't get kicked out for cheating! My dad would be so ashamed! He'd never live it down!"

The kitchen door swung open and Wang's dad came out. With a quick click, Wang closed the *Rapsheet* and switched to the chess association website. Wang's dad glanced at the computer screen, crossed the room and walked down the steps to the store.

"Whew! That was close!" Wang sighed. "I'm only allowed to use the computer on Sunday night for homework—or chess practice."

Josh leaned over Wang and started scrolling down the chess association website.

"You know, I've been thinking about the Binkles," Josh said. "I bet Wilmot's e-mail address is on here somewhere."

Different pages flashed across the screen as Josh clicked through the links, until he got to a list of Association members.

"Here it is: wbinkle at chessassociation dot org."

"I don't see how that's going to help," Magnolia said. "What are you going to do, spam him?"

Wang felt a spark of hope. "Yeah! Something like, 'Beware! Dire doom will befall the Binkles at the Board of Directors' Meeting Sunday! Stay away if you value your lives!'"

Magnolia frowned.

"I don't think they're going to fall for that."

"You know," said Josh, "Wilmot Binkle wasn't such a bad kid."

"What do you mean, not a bad kid?" Wang protested. "He's trying to ruin my life!"

"I don't think he wants you to get kicked out of the chess club. I think it's his dad." Josh turned to Magnolia. "Don't you think so?"

"Yeah," Magnolia agreed. "Wilmot didn't mind losing the game. It was his dad who threw a hairy fit about it."

"You know," Josh continued, "I kind of felt sorry for Wilmot. His dad was really trying to run his life."

"Josh, what are you talking about?" Wang broke in. Feeling sorry for Wilmot was not going to solve Wang's problem.

"Do you remember when we first started Dunces Anonymous?" said Josh. "That notice I put up on the bulletin board?"

"Sure," said Wang. "A club for kids who aren't as good at stuff as their parents think they should be."

"Well, that's Wilmot."

"Are you saying we should invite him into the club?" Wang could hardly believe his ears.

"I think he needs our help." Josh clicked on Wilmot's e-mail and started typing a message. "And you know what? If we get Wilmot on our side, I bet he'll help us too."

The bell rang Monday morning just as Josh was setting foot in the schoolyard. The walk from his mom's condo had taken him longer than usual. He'd been dragging his feet, thinking hard about his plan to recruit Wilmot Binkle, beat the fraudulent-impersonation charge and save Wang from the disgrace of being kicked out of the chess club. He was still deep in thought as he entered the school building among the usual throng of kids. He dropped off his boots and jacket in his locker, climbed the main staircase to the second floor and turned left down the hallway toward Mr. Bogg's classroom. It didn't even cross his mind that this path would take him straight past Emmett Blackwell's locker. In fact, Josh was only a few steps from the locker when he raised his head and caught sight of Emmett. That sight stopped him dead in his tracks.

Emmett's dark hair straggled over his forehead. Black circles ringed his bloodshot eyes. He was standing at the open door of his locker, ripping down the notes from his secret admirer and throwing them in crumpled balls to the floor. Suddenly, he dove into the locker and hauled out the powder blue teddy bear that Wang had planted there, the love poem still pinned to its heart. Emmett clasped the bear's neck in a choke hold and shook it ferociously. Josh took a step backward. At that moment, Emmett turned his head and caught sight of him.

"You!" Emmett rasped. He flung the teddy bear to the ground and leaped toward Josh. Josh spun on his heel, dashed down the hall and dodged through the door into the stairwell.

The stairwell was clogged with a mass of kids heading slowly toward class. Josh spotted a hole in the stream of bodies and deked into it, zigzagging upward through the traffic. He was halfway to the landing when a shout rang out from below.

"Turn, Hellhound, turn!"

Josh turned. Emmett stood in the second-floor doorway, his fists raised in the air. His cry had cleared a path through the stunned students, and now Emmett bounded up the stairs toward Josh. Josh whipped around, but his way upward was blocked by a fat kid who had stopped to tie his shoelace. Josh tried to dart around the kid. Suddenly, he felt himself being tugged backward by a hand grabbing his backpack. Desperately, he slipped his arms out of the shoulder straps and let the backpack fall free. Emmett, caught off balance, stumbled backward into the crowd of kids on the stairs. Boys shouted. Girls screamed. The fat kid straightened up and twisted around to look at the commotion. Josh ducked down and slithered around the fat kid's legs. He sprinted up to the third floor, ran along the hallway, darted down a back staircase and made a dash to the safety of Mr. Bogg's classroom. He burst through the door and slid, panting, into his place in the third row.

Wang rushed over to his desk.

"Hey, Josh, what happened?"

"Emmett Blackwell…he's trying to kill me…," Josh panted.

"Emmett Blackwell!" Wang slapped the desk. "He must have read the *Rapsheet*! He's mad at you for stealing Magnolia!"

"He called me…a Hellhound…"

"Cool! It's just like the Montagues and the Capulets!"

"Cool? Wang, he's crazy! He's a maniac!"

"Listen, Josh." Wang lowered his voice. "You've just got to avoid him for the next couple of days. Just till the dress rehearsal."

"How can I avoid him? He's after me!"

"You've got to go into hiding. Use the back stairways. The subterranean passages!"

"Subterranean passages?" Josh looked at Wang like he was crazy.

"Don't worry," Wang hissed, sliding back to his place as Mr. Bogg appeared in the room. "This is gonna be awesome."

Josh spent the rest of the week sneaking around while Emmett stalked the hallways, looking for revenge. Meanwhile, the gossip about Josh and Magnolia spread through the school like a bad case of chicken pox. Graffiti appeared in the bathroom: *Josh Johnson is a girl mauler.* Kids he didn't even know growled and clawed the air when he passed. He was so preoccupied with dodging Emmet and working out a plan with Wang and Wilmot that he nearly forgot about Stacey Hogarth.

Josh's last class on Friday afternoon was math with Mrs. Singh. It was a short sprint down the hallway from Mrs. Singh's classroom to the gymnasium. At the back of the gymnasium was a small door that opened on to the side of the schoolyard. Hardly anyone except kids who had phys ed last period ever used the door, and they were always late leaving because they had to change out of their gym clothes. It was through this door that Josh intended to make his escape, eluding Emmett Blackwell once and for all.

Two minutes before the end of class, he wriggled into his jacket. When the bell rang, he dumped his math books into his backpack, zipped it shut and raced out the classroom door. A quick dash took him to the door at the back of the gymnasium. He opened it and peeked out.

The coast was clear.

Josh bounded down the steps two at a time. He'd reached the bottom when he heard a voice behind him.

"Aha!"

Josh whirled around. "Stacey!" he exclaimed.

"Who else did you think it was?"

Stacey marched down the stairs and stood on the last step, glaring down at him. She seemed even taller than usual.

"I want to know what's going on," she demanded.

Josh glanced around. The yard was beginning to fill with kids. Soon, Emmett Blackwell would be some-where among them. Instinctively, Josh ducked into the alcove beside the stairway. Stacey followed him.

"You've been avoiding me all week!" she accused.

"No, I haven't," Josh said. It was true; he'd been so busy avoiding Emmett that he hadn't given any thought to avoiding Stacey.

"Admit it! You didn't want to face up to the scandal that you caused by kissing Magnolia."

"Oh, yeah, the scandal! It's huge!" Recovering himself, Josh decided to play up the moment. Now was his chance to get rid of Stacey. "I guess that means that you don't want to join the club anymore."

Stacey guffawed.

"Of course I'm still joining the club, Josh!" she said. "You're the one that should be kicked out!"

Josh took a step backward. His back touched the cold brick wall of the school building. To his right was the concrete staircase and to his left, the chain-link fence of the schoolyard. Looking on the bright side, it was unlikely that Emmet would find him here. On the down side, there was no way to escape Stacey.

"Kicked out of the club?" he gasped.

"It's time for a new president," Stacey declared. "A scandal like this reflects badly on *everyone* in the club."

"But Stacey," said Josh, "you aren't even in the club!"

Stacey's jaw dropped open. "What do you mean, I'm not in the club? I wrote an application letter, just like you said. And besides, you have to let me in the club. It says so in the school rules!"

"I don't care about the rules," Josh shot back. "Because...because it's not even a school club. It's a private club. Members only! And you're not a member!"

Stacey narrowed her eyes.

"If it's not a school club," she said, "then how come your meetings are in Mr. Bogg's classroom?"

"They're not!" Josh retorted, improvising wildly. "Not anymore. Now, they're in...in our private clubhouse!"

"I don't believe you!" Stacey glared at him. "And even if it's true, you still have to let me in. Because if you don't, I'm telling the principal on Wang!"

"On Wang? What for?"

"For setting off the fire alarm. And I know because I saw him running across the teachers' parking lot!"

"You can't tell the principal on Wang!" Josh said. That would be a week's suspension. How could anyone be that mean?

"I can too tell the principal, and I will!" Stacey said. "Unless you let me in the club."

Josh crossed his arms and glared at Stacey. He needed time to think. The situation seemed hopeless.

He couldn't let Stacey tell on Wang—that much was certain. Wang already had to face the board of directors on Sunday. Sure, they had finally worked out a plan with Wilmot, but there was a chance the plan would fail and Wang would be kicked out of the chess club in disgrace. If he got suspended for setting off the fire alarm on top of that, his dad would ground him for life. No, there was no way Josh could let Stacey tell the principal on Wang.

But what choice did he have? To stop Stacey from telling, he had to let her join the club—*and* take over as president. That would be the end of Dunces Anonymous. Josh couldn't let that happen either.

Then Josh saw another possibility.

Sometimes when he was playing chess and he thought he was stumped, he'd suddenly notice a move that he hadn't seen at first. Sometimes the move meant sacrificing a piece, like a rook or a bishop, to protect a more important piece, like the king or the queen.

The move he was contemplating against Stacey would involve a sacrifice too. But it would be worth it to save Wang and the club.

Josh took a deep breath.

"You can't tell the principal on Wang," he said, "because Wang didn't set off the fire alarm. I did."

"You?" This time Stacey took a step backward.

"That's right," Josh said.

"Then how come *he* was running across the parking lot?" said Stacey.

Josh's mind momentarily went blank. He recovered in the next instant.

"Wang's a sword-fighter in the school play," Josh said. "Didn't you know? He's in training."

"In training?" said Stacey.

"Yeah, he runs five miles, every day. So if you're going to tell on anyone," Josh concluded, "you'd better tell on me."

Stacey looked at Josh. He stared back at her, not blinking. Behind her, the schoolyard thronged with students.

"Fine!" she spat. "Then I'll tell on you, Josh!"

"Fine!" he retorted. "Go ahead!"

Stacey turned, her backpack nearly whacking Josh in the face. She marched a few paces and shouted back over her shoulder, "Just wait till Monday, Josh Johnson! You're gonna be in big trouble!"

Stacey whirled away from him again, and Josh watched her ponytail swinging back and forth as she strode into the crowd of kids in the schoolyard. Monday. He might not even survive until Monday. First he, Wang and Magnolia had to pull off Operation Free Juliet at the dress rehearsal on Saturday. Then on Sunday, they had to thwart Mr. Binkle's fraudulent-impersonation charge at the Chess Association board of directors' meeting. If either of those plans backfired, all three of them would be in the soup. Josh sighed, shouldered his backpack and—keeping an eye out for Emmett Blackwell—headed toward the schoolyard exit. It was strangely comforting to think that, by the time Monday rolled around, he might already be in so much trouble that if Stacey told the principal on him, it wouldn't really make any difference.

TWELVE

STAR-CROSSED LOVERS

Girls crowded into the change room at Oakview Public School for the Saturday morning dress rehearsal. There were girls in long dresses and high-heeled silk shoes, girls with elaborate braids and sparkly clips in their hair. All of them were chattering nonstop as they fixed each other's hair and costumes. Magnolia could barely turn around without being stabbed by a safety pin or choked by a cloud of hairspray.

In one corner, a horde of girls swarmed around the rack of dresses from the Drama Club's costume collection. Plastic plates and goblets, spray-painted gold for the Capulets' party scene, lay scattered underfoot.

Magnolia elbowed her way to the dress rack and dug out her costume: a flouncy, floor-length white gown, embroidered with fake diamonds, and a huge silver tiara. Then she staked a place among a crowd of girls in front of the mirror, found a hook to hang up her dress and started putting on her makeup. She'd just finished the left eye and was starting on the right when Hannah Flynn popped out of the thicket of ball gowns and appeared beside her.

"Oh, Magnolia!" Hannah exhaled. "Is it really, truly true that you're going out with *Josh Johnson*?"

"Maybe," said Magnolia, casting Hannah a mysterious look. The scandal had thrown Emmett into a state of confusion, and that confusion could only help Magnolia's plan.

"Emmett is *so* jealous!" said Hannah. "I heard he was going to challenge Josh to a *duel*!"

"I don't believe it!" said Magnolia. The idea of a boy who wore purple knickers dueling anyone seemed ridiculous.

"You're so lucky, Magnolia! You've got two boys fighting over you!" Hannah sighed. "All I want is Emmett, and he won't even look at me!"

Magnolia finished with her eyeliner and shoved the tiara on her head. Then she looked back at her understudy, who was dressed in a sweater and capri pants.

"Hannah, what are you doing? Where's your princess dress?"

"Oh, Magnolia, I'm not wearing a dress. I'm just the understudy!"

Magnolia crossed her arms. This was not going to help their plan at all.

"You have to wear a dress, Hannah! What if I keel over on stage? Then you've got to play Juliet!"

"Do you think you might keel over?" Hannah perked up. "I've practiced really hard! I've memorized my lines and everything! I wouldn't call Romeo a werewolf again, I swear I wouldn't! But"—she pouted—"nothing's going to happen to you, Magnolia!"

"Don't be so sure," said Magnolia darkly. She grabbed Hannah's hand and bushwhacked through the girls in poofy dresses to the dress rack at the back of the change room. The rack was nearly empty, but luckily Hannah was a tiny girl, and a beautiful blue dress in her size, embroidered in glittering jewels, still hung amid the coat hangers.

"Oh, Magnolia, I can't wear this! I'll look just like Juliet!" Hannah breathed, fingering the velvety fabric.

"Hannah, you dodo, you're *supposed* to look like Juliet!"

"Oh, yeah." Hannah hugged the dress. "I guess you're right."

Magnolia helped Hannah into her dress and styled her hair in romantic ringlets. She added pink lip gloss, eye shadow and a touch of mascara, then stepped back to admire Hannah's transformation into the perfect Juliet. Magnolia nodded, just as Mrs. Karloff came into the change room, calling, "Five minutes, girls! Five minutes to curtain!"

The girls poured out of the dressing room. Magnolia hustled Hannah backstage and planted her beside Josh, who was standing by the pull-cord, waiting to open the curtains.

"Now stay here," Magnolia instructed Hannah. "And if anything happens to me, remember, *you're* Juliet!"

Squeezing around Josh, Magnolia peeked out into the gymnasium from behind the curtain. The chairs had already been set up, row upon row, where the audience would sit on the night of the show. The chairs were empty now, except for the one in the middle of the front row where Magnolia's mother sat, flowered scarves draped around her neck, awaiting the beginning of the performance.

Magnolia took a deep breath. Everything depended on this: Could she act convincingly enough to fool her mother? What if she flubbed it? What if she forgot her lines? She couldn't allow that to happen! Operation Free Juliet mustn't fail now. It was her only chance.

"Two minutes, people! Two minutes!" Mrs. Karloff called. A whispered commotion ran through the crowd backstage as girls adjusted their high-heeled shoes and boys searched for their swords in the piles of props. "One minute!" The lights in the gymnasium went off, silence fell, the stage lights came up and Josh, heaving on the rope, swept the curtains open.

The play began with a fight scene between Romeo's family, the Montagues, and Juliet's family, the Capulets. From backstage, Magnolia watched Wang's performance in admiration. He was an acrobatic sword-fighter, jumping and rolling to avoid his enemies' blades, then leaping to his feet to thrust and parry with his own weapon. The scene ended when the prince came onstage to break up the fight and warn that anyone else caught fighting would be sentenced to death.

The action continued through the party scene, where Romeo first met Juliet and fell in love with her. When Emmett came to the line about giving Juliet a "tender kiss," his lips swooped close to hers. He'll do it for real on performance night, Magnolia thought. She shuddered. Operation Free Juliet *had* to work.

The party scene ended. Next was the balcony scene. As she waited for her cue to enter, Magnolia rehearsed her lines in her head. This was it—the moment when all would be revealed. Magnolia looked around to make sure everyone was in place. Hannah beside Josh on the edge of the stage. Check. Emmett sneaking through Juliet's garden on the way to her balcony. Check. Magnolia's mom enraptured by the action. Check.

"'Oh, that I were a glove upon that hand, that I might touch that cheek!'" Emmett sighed, gazing up at her balcony.

That was Magnolia's cue. She stepped out and delivered her first line.

"Emmett, you've been living a lie!"

Emmett stepped backward. He looked like he'd been hit on the head with a sledgehammer.

"Huh?" he spluttered.

Magnolia continued. "I know you love me, Emmett. I've seen it in your eyes. In the way you look at me across a crowded room. I know your heart is burning with passion. But, alas! I cannot love you the same way!"

With a sweep of her princess dress, Magnolia jumped from the balcony and landed in front of Emmett.

He took another a step backward, stunned.

"It's no use pretending, Emmett. It's no use going on like this!" she cried. "All the time that you've been yearning for me, another girl has loved you with a true and faithful heart! Someone a hundred times more worthy of your love than I am! Yes, Emmett, your Secret Admirer!"

"My Secret Admirer!" Emmett gasped. "Who is she?"

At that moment, Josh nudged Hannah in the back. Off balance in her high-heeled shoes, Hannah stumbled onstage.

"You!" Emmett exclaimed.

"Me?" Hannah breathed.

"The poems, the gifts, the flowers!" Emmett cried.

"The poems, the gifts, the flowers?" Hannah repeated.

"I cannot tear these two young hearts asunder!" Magnolia announced. She lifted the sparkly tiara from her head and placed it on Hannah's. "Hannah, you are Emmett's true Juliet."

"Oh, Magnolia!" Hannah turned to her, eyes filled with tears. "I couldn't!"

"You must, Hannah!" Magnolia insisted. "You and Emmett are meant to be together! Nothing can stand in the way of True Love!"

At that moment, Magnolia's mother burst into tears.

"Bravo! Bravo!" she applauded, rising from her chair.

But Mrs. Karloff's voice blared like a siren from the back of the gymnasium. "Magnolia Montcrieff! What in the name of the Immortal Bard of Avon is the meaning of this?"

Magnolia froze as Mrs. Karloff's high heels drummed across the gymnasium floor, getting louder and louder as she approached. The drama teacher pounded up the stairs into the glare of the stage lights. Her eyes gleamed like daggers.

"I was handing over the role of Juliet to Hannah." Magnolia mustered her courage under Mrs. Karloff's stare. "She and Emmett are fated to be together!"

"Actors do not *hand over* roles!" Mrs. Karloff huffed. "Directors *hand over* roles. And, as you appear to have forgotten, *I* am the director of this play! For the past six weeks, Magnolia, I have coached you on every 'whence' and 'wherefore' of Shakespeare's romantic masterpiece, and I expect you to stand up and deliver your lines on performance night. Is that clear?"

Mrs. Karloff glared at her.

"You...you mean Hannah can't play Juliet?" Magnolia stuttered.

"Thank you for your insight, Magnolia. That is exactly what I mean!"

"But, it's True Love!" Magnolia and her mom exclaimed simultaneously.

"True Love!" Mrs. Karloff threw her hands in the air. "Magnolia, darling, I am trying to put on a production of *Romeo and Juliet* with a pack of semi-literate middle graders. I can assure you that True Love is the furthest thing from my mind. Now, will you take your place, please? We'll start at 'What light through yonder window breaks.'" Mrs. Karloff clapped her hands briskly and spun on her heel. "All right. When you're ready!"

Magnolia shot a despairing glance at Josh. She looked at her mother, sitting in the front row, sobbing into a handkerchief. They had come so close. Everything would have been perfect if it hadn't been for Mrs. Karloff. Then a voice rang out, clear, loud and confident.

"No!"

Emmett Blackwell stepped forward.

"No?" Mrs. Karloff turned to him. "What do you mean, *No*?"

"No! I cannot play Romeo if Magnolia is Juliet!" Emmett swept a hand to his forehead. "Yes, once I thought I loved her! But it was a cruel deception! Hannah is my true love!"

"Emmett, what sort of folly is this?"

"No folly, Mrs. Karloff, but the sweet folly of love! If Magnolia stays, I go!"

Mrs. Karloff looked at Emmett, then at Hannah, who was on the verge of tears in her oversized silver tiara, and then at Magnolia. She threw up her hands in disgust.

"All right! Have it your way! Emmett, Hannah, the balcony scene! Now! And I want you here for three-hour rehearsals every afternoon until the performance! Magnolia, you clean up that mess backstage! And there had better not be one thing out of place on performance night because if anyone—anyone—walks out onstage without their props in hand, you will never act in a play at Oakview Public School again, Magnolia Montcrieff!"

Mrs. Karloff turned on her spiky heel and thundered down the stage stairs. Josh slumped in relief against the wall backstage. Emmett swept Hannah into his arms. Magnolia's mother wept into her handkerchief.

"True Love, my foot!" Mrs. Karloff exclaimed as she strode toward the back of the gymnasium. "Next year I'm staging a murder mystery!"

"A murder mystery," Magnolia repeated under her breath, as she tiptoed downstage and descended the steps to the gymnasium floor. She crept over to her mother and put her arm around her shoulders, weaving her hand through the flowery scarves. Her mom was still sniffling, whether over the romance of the situation or the fact that her daughter would no longer be playing Juliet, Magnolia wasn't sure.

"Don't be upset, Mom," she whispered as the balcony scene resumed onstage. "There's always next year's play. And you know what? I think I'd make a pretty good murderer."

THIRTEEN

THE BOARD OF DIRECTORS

Wang sat in the car's front passenger seat on Sunday morning, watching out the window as they sped along the highway toward the Traveler's Repose Hotel. Next to him in the driver's seat sat his dad, stony silent, eyes locked on the road. He'd hardly said a word to Wang since the night before, when he'd found out about the board of directors' meeting.

Wang had been planning to attend the meeting alone and, hopefully, never tell his parents about it at all. But his dad had discovered the secret when Mrs. Singh, the teacher who organized the school chess club, had called Wang's house to make sure they knew the time and place of the meeting.

"But Dad! What Mr. Binkle says about me—it's not true!" Wang had protested when his father put down the phone. His dad had only looked at him and said, "We'll see." His stern expression put an end to the conversation—temporarily. If the board of directors found him guilty of lying and cheating, Wang didn't even want to think about what his dad would say.

Josh's plan had better work, thought Wang. Or I am dead. Really, really dead.

They turned into the parking lot of the Traveler's Repose Hotel, parked the car and walked silently through the main doors into the lobby. Wang looked around. He'd expected a meeting at a hotel to be more glamorous, with a red carpet and a chandelier hanging from the ceiling and a valet to open the door and say, "Allow me to escort you to your room, sir." But the lobby of the Traveler's Repose looked pretty much like a doctor's waiting room, only bigger. There was a counter where people checked in, a few brown chairs grouped into a square, and some newspapers and magazines lying around on coffee tables.

His dad strode toward a board, where the day's events were listed, and scanned it. He nodded once, without speaking and set off up the stairs. Wang trailed behind him.

The meeting room was filled with rows of chairs with scratchy-looking seats, all facing the front, where a long rectangular table stood on an elevated platform. That was where the board of directors was supposed to sit, Wang guessed—the people who would decide if he was guilty or innocent. At the back of the room was a long table filled with trays of donuts. Wang's stomach growled, but he knew his dad wouldn't let him have any. This was much too serious an occasion for donuts.

The room was full of adults who were talking, piling donuts onto little Styrofoam plates and bumping into each other as they tried to get to their seats. In the center of one of the rows, nearly hidden among the adults, Wang saw two kids—Josh and Magnolia, he guessed, though both of them were wearing disguises so that no one would recognize them. Magnolia wore a big pair of dark sunglasses and a blond wig that reached down to her waist. Josh had a baseball cap pulled down over his eyes, while the rest of his face was hidden by the book he was pretending to read—*Strategic Algorithms: Learning the Chess Secrets of the Masters.*

Wang wished he could run over and talk to them, but he tore his eyes away instead. Even looking at them could arouse suspicion, he reminded himself. Everything would be lost if he blew their cover.

Wang's dad walked straight to the front of the room and found two empty chairs in the very first row. He sat down stiffly. Wang sat beside him but not before noticing that another boy and his father were sitting a little farther down the row. They were both wearing navy blue suits and ties: the father looked angry, the boy uncomfortable. They must be Wilmot Binkle and his father, Wang guessed. Wilmot, just as Josh had described him, was sweating.

The people in the room settled into their chairs and their voices died down as the five members of the board of directors took their seats at the head table. Wang's watch read exactly 9:00 AM when the man sitting in the center of the table—obviously the chairman of the board—banged his wooden gavel and called the meeting to order.

The chairman had a square jaw, large square-rimmed glasses and a thick thatch of bushy brown hair. He wore a brown jacket and a brown tie, and at the end of each agenda item, he whacked his gavel on the table and barked "Next item!" in a businesslike voice.

Wang swallowed hard. He imagined the chairman banging his gavel and shouting "Guilty! Next item!" at the end of his fraudulent-impersonation hearing. He imagined being grabbed by the elbows by two other members of the board and marched out of the room, under the stern and shame-filled eyes of his father. Wang snuck a peek at Wilmot Binkle, but the sight of the sweaty pink-faced kid wasn't reassuring. Denial and confusion—that was the essence of their plan. They'd worked it out with Wilmot by e-mail and text messaging over the past week, but Wang had never seen Wilmot face-to-face until today. What if the plan went wrong? What if Wilmot had second thoughts? Why had he entrusted his life to a perfect stranger?

Wang himself was feeling less and less confident about his ability to carry out their plan. It had been one thing when his dad didn't know about the board of directors' meeting, when Wang was supposed to be here alone. But now his father was sitting right in front, listening to everything, witnessing everything. Could he really get up there and lie in front of everyone— in front of his own dad?

"Next item!" The chairman banged his gavel on the table, after finishing a discussion of the purchase of new chess sets for underprivileged schools.

"An allegation of fraudulent impersonation brought against Wang Xiu by Wilmot Binkle and his father. Could Wang and Wilmot now come forward, please!"

Wang glanced at his dad, who motioned him to get up. Then he looked over at Wilmot Binkle, who was already edging toward the head table. Wang felt his knees shaking as he rose from his seat. This is no time to panic, he told himself.

The chairman peered at Wang and Wilmot through his large square-rimmed glasses; then he motioned them to sit on two chairs on the elevated platform. As they sat down, Wang shot another glance at Wilmot, who had a look of panic in his eye, like someone had hurled a dodgeball at him and he couldn't get out of the way fast enough. Drops of sweat beaded on his forehead.

"You're Wilmot Binkle?" said the chairman, turning toward him.

"Yes, sir."

"And do you have a parent or legal guardian present in the room who can vouch for your identity?"

"Yes, sir, that's my dad over there."

As Wilmot pointed, his father rose from his seat in the front row. One of the board members left his chair and went over to check Mr. Binkle's identification.

Then the chairman nodded and turned to Wang.

"And you are Wang Xiu?"

"Yes, sir." Wang's voice shook.

"And do you have a parent or legal guardian present in the room who can vouch for your identity?"

"Yes, sir." Wang turned toward his father, who was sitting very straight, his eyes fixed on the chairman, creases tracing a line from his cheekbones to the down-turned corners of his mouth. Now, he rose and bowed toward the chairman. The board member checked his identification too and nodded.

"Very well. Now that we've established that you boys are, indeed, who you say you are, let's turn to the matter at hand. The allegation of fraudulent impersonation during the Centennial Fall Chess Tournament." The chairman pinned Wang with his eyes, which seemed magnified in both size and power by his glasses.

"Now, Wang, is it a fact that you were registered in the Centennial Fall Chess Tournament this October?"

Wang opened his mouth, but it was too dry to speak. He felt the blood drain from his face and go rushing through his heart, to form a sickening pool in the pit of his stomach. He could feel his dad's eyes upon him. Registered to attend? Well, that was true at least. He was *registered*. Wang licked his lips and turned to face the chairman.

"Yes, sir," he croaked.

"And you were scheduled to play a match against this boy sitting opposite you, Wilmot Binkle?"

The pit of Wang's stomach burned. Scheduled? Well, it was true that he was *scheduled* to play Wilmot.

"Yes, sir," Wang squeaked again.

"Now, Wang, we get to the crux of the matter." The chairman leaned toward him. Wang didn't want to look at his father, but he couldn't help himself. It was as though a powerful force was making him turn his head toward the audience. Wang's eyes locked on to his father's. His father stared back at him, his gaze seeming to penetrate into Wang's very soul. Wang couldn't lie, he knew he couldn't.

"Tell me truthfully," the chairman said, "did you or did you not send another boy to the tournament to play in your place in order to improve your chess ranking?"

"Oh no, sir!" Wang exclaimed. He was so relieved to be telling the truth that the words gushed out of him. "No, truly, I didn't! I couldn't care less about the chess ranking! Really!"

"Hmmm." The chairman studied his face for a long moment, then nodded and turned his attention toward Wilmot. Wang slumped back in his chair as though he'd just been released from an iron grip. The blood rushed from his stomach back to his brain, thundering like a river torrent in his ears. He looked at his father, but his father was no longer looking at him. Instead his attention was fixed on the chairman, who was now interrogating Wilmot Binkle, asking him if he had attended the Centennial tournament, and if he had played a match against a boy named Wang Xiu. Wang snapped back to his senses. He wasn't safe yet. His life still depended on Wilmot's answers.

"Now Wilmot," said the chairman sternly, as Wang focused his attention on the proceedings. "Look carefully at this boy sitting here, Wang Xiu, and tell me, is this the same boy you played at the Centennial Fall Chess Tournament? Or was that boy, in fact, an imposter?"

Wang looked at Wilmot. His round face, already shiny with perspiration, broke into a new flood of sweat. He opened and closed his mouth several times, like a fish taken out of its bowl. Denial and confusion, Wang urged him mentally, wishing for telepathic powers. Finally, Wilmot choked out an answer: "I don't really know what to say, sir."

The chairman tapped his index finger impatiently on the table.

"You don't know what to say?"

"No," Wilmot gasped.

"What exactly do you mean by that?"

"I mean...I mean, I want to withdraw the charges," Wilmot blubbered. "I mean, I never wanted to get anyone into trouble!"

"You wish to withdraw the charges?" The chairman drew his eyebrows together in a frown.

Wilmot nodded.

Wang felt like hugging him, sweat and all.

At that moment, Wilmot's father jumped from his seat. "Preposterous!" he thundered. "Outrageous! Scandalous! Egregious! Unbelievable!"

"Mr. Binkle! Order!" The chairman whammed his gavel on the table. "You will please wait for the Chair to recognize you before speaking!"

"Order? Order be hanged!" Mr. Binkle shouted. "Why, I was there! I saw the boy who beat my son! This boy looks nothing like him! This is nothing but... but...intimidation!"

"Very well, Mr. Binkle! You've had your say." The chairman hammered his gavel on the table until Wilmot's dad sat down, fuming, in his seat.

"Now, Wilmot," continued the chairman, turning toward the boy, "this is a very serious matter. First, you brought a complaint of fraudulent impersonation against Wang, and now you say that you wish to withdraw the charges. If you weren't sure, Wilmot, why did you bring the complaint in the first place?"

The chairman peered at Wilmot through his square glasses. Wilmot lowered his eyes and shot an unhappy glance toward his father. It looked like he was crying, Wang realized. But with all the sweat on his face, it was hard to tell.

"Because...," Wilmot stammered, "because my dad was mad at me for losing the game."

The chairman sat for a moment without saying anything. Silence fell on the room. Slowly, the chairman spoke: "According to the chess club Constitution, a complaint may be brought by a member of the club in conjunction with a parent or guardian, but the parent or guardian may not bring a complaint alone. In other words, the club member must always be involved. In this case, as young Wilmot has sincerely expressed his desire to withdraw the complaint, I must dismiss the charge of fraudulent impersonation."

The chairman banged the gavel and declared, "Next item!"

Relief gushed over Wang like a waterfall. He turned to his father, who rose and acknowledged the chairman's verdict with a deep, respectful bow.

Mr. Binkle sprang up and stormed out of the room, shouting curses as he left and completely forgetting his son, who sat like a wet dishcloth in his chair on the dais.

But Wang stood up and reached out his hand to shake Wilmot Binkle's.

Wang's father said nothing as Wang returned to his place in the front row. He only stared at him with a grave and thoughtful look that made Wang lower his eyes to the floor. Finally, he said, "Let's go," and they left the meeting room, retraced their steps through the lobby and back to the parking lot. Wang's father didn't speak again until the car was well out of the parking lot and heading down the highway, back toward town.

"The store needs sweeping and mopping today," he said, staring straight ahead at the traffic and not turning to glance at Wang.

That caught Wang off guard. He'd expected a discussion about the board of directors' meeting, not a work assignment.

"Aw, Dad!"

Wang had stocked the shelves yesterday evening. Usually one big chore was enough on weekends.

"The refrigerators for the green groceries have to be cleaned out," his dad continued. "Then you can finish by washing the windows."

Wang opened his mouth to protest. Cleaning out the refrigerators! Washing the windows! Those weren't just chores—that was punishment! Punishment. That thought made Wang immediately close his mouth. He snuck a look at his dad's face but couldn't read it. He seemed intent on the traffic ahead.

Wang felt the burning return to the pit of his stomach. He wished he could ask his dad how much he knew about what had happened at the tournament. Maybe Dad thought Wang really had sent Josh there to improve his chess ranking, and this was his punishment for it. That would be the worst! But on the other hand, maybe he didn't suspect anything. Maybe he just really wanted the store cleaned out. Maybe, Wang thought miserably, the best thing to do was to keep his mouth shut. He leaned his forehead against the window and looked out. They passed some car dealerships and superstores with huge parking lots. The sky was gray but it wasn't raining. The air in the car smelled stale.

"I think," his dad said finally, as though musing out loud, "that if someone wanted to send someone else to a chess tournament to improve their ranking, they would not send a beginner who would win only one game."

"That's right, Dad!" exclaimed Wang, turning toward him hopefully. "That's true!"

"So, perhaps," his dad continued, still not looking at Wang, but at the road ahead, "someone might send someone else to play for them at a chess tournament if they were very busy that day. Busy with something very important."

"Yes! They would! They might!" Wang agreed.

"Still," Wang's dad continued, bringing the car to a stop at a stoplight and turning to look directly at Wang, "it would not be right for that person to lie to his parents about it."

"I know, Dad." Wang met his father's eye; then he hung his head. "I...I had fencing practice for the school play. I thought if I asked, you'd make me go to the chess tournament instead."

"Fencing?" The traffic light turned green, and his dad put the car in gear, turning his eyes back to the road.

"It's a kind of sword-fighting, Dad. All the Capulets have to learn it. See, the Capulets are Juliet's family and they're locked in a deadly feud with Romeo's family, the Montagues. And I'm a Capulet in the play! And Declan's dad says I'm a natural."

"Sword-fighting in a play," his dad repeated. He seemed unconvinced that this was an important enough reason for missing a chess tournament.

"But fencing is more than that!" Wang exclaimed. "It's really great. It teaches you concentration and discipline and strategy and everything. And I'd...I'd really like to take lessons, Dad. Really."

"Lessons." His dad put on the turn signal and veered off the main road and into their neighborhood. "How will you have time for lessons? You already complain that you don't have time to get all your schoolwork done."

"But Dad! I'll do my schoolwork if you let me take fencing lessons! I bet my marks will even get better!"

"You take chess lessons and your marks don't get better," his dad answered.

"But I hate chess, Dad!" Wang blurted. "How can something I hate improve my marks?"

His dad frowned.

"Discipline will improve your marks."

"Fencing teaches discipline, Dad. Really! Can't you come to just one lesson and see? Can't we just try?"

His dad turned left onto their street and drove slowly past the familiar restaurants and bubble-tea shops. Neighbors with shopping bags bustled down the sidewalks.

"Today you have a lot of work to do in the store," his dad said finally. "Do it well, and tomorrow we will look into these fencing lessons."

"Dad, you're the greatest!"

Wang felt like jumping out of the car, running the rest of the way to the store and grabbing the big, heavy stiff-bristled broom right away to start sweeping. The store would be the cleanest his parents had ever seen it, he vowed. And in his heart he also vowed that he would never keep the truth from his father again.

Not unless it was an *absolute* emergency.

FOURTEEN

PRESIDENT JOSH

Josh hung up the phone in the living room. It was one thirty on Monday afternoon.

"She said to sit right here and not move until she gets home."

"Was she mad?" said Wang.

Josh nodded.

"Really mad?"

"Really mad."

Josh pulled his knees up to his chin and wrapped his arms around his legs. His bum sank into the leather cushion of the sofa. He stared straight ahead—looking at the fake logs in the electric fireplace—and not at

Wang and Magnolia, who were sitting in the black leather chairs on either side.

Josh appreciated Wang and Magnolia skipping their afternoon classes to be here with him when his mom came home. Josh wasn't skipping school—at least, not by choice. The principal had sent him home to start serving his suspension immediately. It was meant, he said, to impress upon Josh the seriousness of wantonly pulling the school fire alarm.

"Maybe we could think of a cunning plan?" Wang suggested in a small voice.

"In the next ten minutes?" said Magnolia.

"Forget it, you guys," said Josh. "I'm just gonna have to take it."

"You shouldn't have confessed in my place, Josh," said Wang.

"It was my idea, the whole Operation Juliet thing," said Josh. "Why should you be the one who gets in trouble?"

He rested his chin on his knees and listened for the sound of his mother's arrival. For a long time there was nothing to hear but the hum of the fridge in the kitchen and the muffled sounds of traffic on the street outside. It was a twenty-five-minute walk from his mom's office to the condo. Josh looked at the second hand on his wristwatch, sweeping through the minutes, a full circle each. Then he heard the elevator—its *ting, ting, ting,* getting louder as it stopped at each floor—and finally the loudest *ting,* just down the hallway, and the *whoosh* of the doors opening to let someone off.

There was no sound of footfalls. A thick carpet covered the hallway floor. Josh bit his lip and counted seconds—one, two, three, four, five, six, seven, eight. Then came the soft, gliding sound of the pass-card and the magnetic click of the door unlocking. A second later, his mother appeared in the living-room doorway.

Her face was flushed from the cold. She grasped her winter hat in one hand. Strands of her hair, stiffened with hairspray, stuck out from her head. Her long winter coat was unbuttoned halfway, and she was still wearing her tall winter boots, which she normally took off before setting foot inside the condo. A pool of slush was forming at her feet.

"Young man," she said, "you have got some serious explaining to do."

Josh looked at the dead fireplace.

"I got suspended," he said.

"I know you got suspended! For crying out loud, Josh, your principal called me in the middle of a meeting!" His mother threw her hat down on the coffee table. "You know, Josh, I work pretty hard so that you can live in a nice neighborhood and go to a good school, so how do you think it feels when the principal tells me that my son has just been suspended for a week for deliberately setting off the school fire alarm?"

Josh shrugged and stuck his nose in the crook between his knees.

"It feels like I've done something wrong as a parent, that's how it feels." His mother paced to the living-room window, leaving a trail of wet pointy-toed footprints behind her. She turned to face him.

"And you call yourself a Young Leader of the Future!"

"But Mom, I didn't!" The protest broke from Josh's throat, even though he'd vowed to say nothing and to accept his punishment silently.

"Didn't what? Didn't set off the school fire alarm?" She put her hands on her hips.

"Didn't call myself a Young Leader of the Future," Josh muttered.

"Josh, what on earth are you talking about?"

"The club, Mom." Josh raised his eyes to look at her.

"The club! What has the club got to do with this?"

"Everything! You don't understand!" Josh shouted. "And it's *not* the Young Leaders of the Future! It's… it's…Dunces Anonymous!"

For a moment the room was silent. Wang and Magnolia sat frozen in their armchairs. Josh's mom stared at him with her hands still on her hips. She turned and looked out the window for a second. Then she whirled back and looked at him.

"And what is Dunces Anonymous? Some sort of club for young delinquents who go around setting off school fire alarms?"

"That was an accident!" Wang burst out, jumping from his chair. Josh's mom turned toward him, as though noticing him for the first time.

"And besides," Wang continued, "it wasn't Josh who set off the fire alarm. It was me."

"Josh, is this true?" his mother looked at him.

Josh nodded.

"And who is this?" his mother demanded.

"That's Wang," Josh explained miserably. "He's in the club."

Josh's mother turned toward Wang again.

"Well, Wang-who's-in-the-club, don't you think that you should have told the principal about this yourself, instead of letting your friend get in trouble?"

"But he couldn't!" This time it was Magnolia who interrupted, jumping up from the other armchair. "His dad would have grounded him for life! And besides, he only did it to stop Emmett Blackwell from kissing me. Right on the lips!"

Josh's mom looked at Magnolia. Then she looked at Wang. Then she looked at Josh. Then she walked across the living room, sat down on a footstool, unzipped her right boot and pulled it off.

"And you are…?" she said finally, setting the boot down on the floor.

"Magnolia," Josh said. "She's in the club too."

"The club." Josh's mom bent to unzip her other boot. "The infamous club."

She pulled off her left boot and set it next to the right.

"So let me get this straight." She turned to Josh. "This friend of yours, Wang, set off the fire alarm to stop this other friend of yours from getting kissed by a boy. And you confessed to it, so that Wang wouldn't get in trouble with his dad. Because he's in your club."

"Yeah," said Josh. "That's about it."

Josh's mom closed her eyes and pressed her hand to her forehead. She drew her fingers along the furrows on her brow. Then she opened her eyes again.

"Well, Josh," she said, "at least you acted like a president."

"I did?" Josh looked up.

"Presidents take responsibility for other people's actions," she said. "That's what leadership is about."

"Does that mean you're not mad at me?"

"I don't know, Josh. I don't know what to think." His mother stood up and unbuttoned her coat. She was staring at a corner of the room, half turned away from Josh. Then she walked over to where he was sitting, slung her coat over the arm of the sofa and sat down next to him.

"Why did you lie to me about the club?" she said.

"I didn't mean to, Mom," Josh said, "but you were so disappointed when I lost the election, and I wanted to cheer you up so I told you I started a club, and you wanted me to call it the Young Leaders of the Future, so I just sort of went along with it."

Josh looked at his mom. She was sitting very close to him, and he could see that her lipstick had worn off, leaving her lips pale and faded. There were little lines all around her mouth, as though her lips had shrunk, drawing in the skin. She looked tired and kind of sad.

"I didn't want you to think I was a loser," he added.

"Oh, Josh. Of course I don't think you're a loser." He felt her pick up a strand of hair behind his ear and twirl it in her finger, the way she used to do when he was little.

"I just want you to be the best that you can be," she said.

"But how can I be the best at something if I don't even like it?"

"I thought you liked student politics," she said.

"I don't like it, Mom. *You* like it."

She nodded and twirled his hair some more.

"Okay, Josh," she said finally. "Is there anything else you don't like that I should know about, before you and your friends go setting off more school fire alarms?"

Josh hesitated.

"You're going to be mad at me," he said.

"Come on, Josh. Why would I be mad at you for telling the truth?"

Josh wondered about that question. People got mad at him all the time for telling the truth. Otherwise, he'd never have to lie, and he'd been doing a lot of lying in the past couple of months. Still, she said she wanted the truth.

"Well, it's about your cooking..."

"My gourmet dinners?" His mom pulled back.

"I knew you were going to be mad!"

"But Josh, I work hard at those dinners. It's our only time together, as a family. Why don't you want it to be special?"

Now she didn't look mad anymore. She looked like she was going to cry.

"I do, Mom! It can still be special. We can...we can..." Josh felt himself floundering and looked to Wang and Magnolia for help.

"You can eat by candlelight!" Magnolia interjected.

"Yeah, eat by candlelight!" Josh said. He didn't know why that would be special, but maybe it was something that girls liked. "And I can help you cook sometimes," he added. "Maybe we could make hamburgers."

"Hamburgers by candlelight?" His mom sounded doubtful.

"Candlelight for you and hamburgers for me. That way it'd be special for both of us."

His mother's lips curved up a little. It wasn't a full smile but it was a start.

"Okay, Josh. I guess you've made your point," she said. "But if you don't like student politics and you don't like my gourmet cooking, what *do* you like?"

Josh thought about that for a minute.

"You know what, Mom? I think I like chess."

"Not chess!" Wang moaned, falling backward into his armchair.

Josh grinned. "Yeah, I think I'll join the chess club," he said.

He gave his mom a big smile.

"In fact, I might just run for president."

EPILOGUE

A NEW MEMBER

Josh rapped the small wooden mallet on the coffee table.

"Okay, you guys, this meeting will now come to order!"

Josh looked around the living room. Magnolia was lolling in one of the black leather chairs, her feet dangling over the armrest. Sitting in the other chair, and looking as though he wished he could disappear beneath the cushion like a piece of loose pocket change, was Wilmot Binkle. Josh smiled at him encouragingly. Then he looked over at Wang, who was practicing fencing with a bulrush that he'd plucked from a dried flower arrangement in the corner.

"Wang!"

"Oh, sorry!" Wang leaned against the windowsill and swung the bulrush down by his side.

"Right," Josh continued, now that everyone was paying attention. "Has anyone got anything to report?"

"Well," said Magnolia, "my mom lo-o-o-ved the school play." She rolled her eyes.

"She wasn't upset that you didn't get to play Juliet?" said Josh.

"She got over it. She said it was Destiny that brought Emmett and Hannah together."

"That wasn't Destiny," Wang interjected. "That was our cunning plan!"

"*I* know that, and *you* know that, but *she* doesn't know that," Magnolia answered. "Anyway, now I just have to convince her to let me try out for the part of the murderer in next year's play."

"The murderer!" Wang exclaimed, stabbing an invisible opponent with his dried bulrush.

"What if the murderer also has to kiss someone?" Josh said. Magnolia kicked her feet idly.

"I guess it wouldn't be *so* bad," she reflected, "if I got to murder him afterward."

Wang resumed his fencing practice, trying to out-parry a potted plant that sat in front of the window.

"Well, my parents loved the play too," he said between thrusts. "And guess what? You're never going to believe this!"

Wang paused to deliver a deathblow to the potted plant.

"Believe what?" Josh prodded him.

Wang turned away from his victim. "After he saw me in the play, my dad agreed to pay for fencing lessons."

"That's great, Wang!" said Magnolia.

"Yeah. Dad says he hopes it teaches me honor and discipline. And he said he'll think about letting me quit the chess club. Sorry, Josh."

"That's okay." Josh looked over at Wilmot, who was hunkered silently in his chair. "Wilmot and I can practice together, right, Wil?"

Wilmot looked up. "Yeah."

The word fell from his lips like a lead weight.

"Hey, Wil, what's wrong?" said Josh.

"Oh, never mind. You'll think it's stupid."

"Come on, Wil," Magnolia urged him. "You can tell us. You're part of the club now."

"Yeah," added Wang, "you're one of us!"

"You guys are going to laugh." Wilmot hung his head. "But I don't really like chess. What I really want to do is...is play electric guitar."

"Electric guitar!" Wang exclaimed.

"That's not stupid. That's awesome!" said Magnolia.

"It doesn't matter anyway." Wilmot sighed. "My dad'll never let me."

"Your dad?" Magnolia swung her feet down from the armrest and planted them on the floor. "We can't let your dad stand in your way."

"We can't? But…"

Wang brandished his bulrush. "What we need is a cunning plan," he announced.

"A cunning plan?" Wilmot looked at Josh. Sweat was starting to break out on his forehead.

Josh walked over to the armchair and put his hand on Wilmot's shoulder.

"Don't worry, Wil," he said. "Just leave everything to Dunces Anonymous."

ACKNOWLEDGMENTS

First and foremost, I would like to thank my writing colleague Mark Baker, who gave me the idea for this book and came up with the title. Without him, *Dunces Anonymous* would not exist. I am grateful to Mark and the other members of my writing group—Noreen Violetta, Connie Topper, Rachel Eugster, Michelle Jodoin and Deborah Jackson—for their feedback throughout the writing process. Their input helped me to turn an awkward and unfinished first draft into something presentable. Immense thanks are due to my editor, Sarah Harvey, who helped me to wrestle down some difficult issues of plot and point of view. Her editorial advice greatly improved the manuscript.

As always, I would like to thank my loving and supportive family. Thanks to my father Jim for renovating an old laundry room in the basement so that I could have a writing room; to my mother Ann for literary enthusiasm and encouragement; to my sister Bobbi for inspiring me not to give up on crazy dreams; to my brother Charles for saying the manuscript was great and anyone who didn't want to publish it had no taste in literature; and to my brother-in-law Kit for all his work on my website. Deep and abiding thanks go out to my husband Mark for his love and support. I would also like to acknowledge my daughters Zoey and Molly, who always know how to make me smile and who served as models for the character Garland in this book.

KATE JAIMET developed an early taste for madcap plotlines due to childhood exposure to the novels of P.G. Wodehouse. Kate studied literature at the University of Toronto and has a degree in journalism from Ryerson University. Now a reporter at the *Ottawa Citizen*, Kate spends much of her time trying to keep one step ahead of her two young daughters. Visit her website at www.katejaimet.com.